Killa Kounty 2

Khufu

Lock Down Publications and Ca$h
Presents

Killa Kounty 2
A Novel by *Khufu*

Khufu

Lock Down Publications
P.O. Box 944
Stockbridge, Ga 30281

Visit our website @
www.lockdownpublications.com

Lock Down Publications
Like our page on Facebook: Lock Down Publications @
www.facebook.com/lockdownpublications.ldp

Book interior design by: **Shawn Walker**
Edited by: **Lashonda Johnson**

Stay Connected with Us!

Text **LOCKDOWN** to 22828 to stay up-to-date with new releases, sneak peaks, contests and more...
Thank you.

Submission Guideline.

Submit the first three chapters of your completed manuscript to ldpsubmissions@gmail.com, subject line: Your book's title. The manuscript must be in a .doc file and sent as an attachment. Document should be in Times New Roman, double spaced and in size 12 font. Also, provide your synopsis and full contact information. If sending multiple submissions, they must each be in a separate email.

Have a story but no way to send it electronically? You can still submit to LDP/Ca$h Presents. Send in the first three chapters, written or typed, of your completed manuscript to:

LDP: Submissions Dept
P.O. Box 944
Stockbridge, Ga 30281

DO NOT send original manuscript. Must be a duplicate.

Provide your synopsis and a cover letter containing your full contact information.

Thanks for considering LDP and Ca$h Presents.

Dedication

I dedicate this book to my son—AJ—and all my niggaz with life sentences—Quinten Bradely, C-Rock, Jimmy Reeves, Lil' Keedy, and Killa.
Rest In Power.
Stacey, Tela, and Tayda—
I love y'all forever!

Acknowledgements

First and foremost, I thank you, the Almighty! Without you nothing is tangible. To Ca$h and Lock Down Publication, I appreciate you for turning my conception into a reality. My appreciation for this opportunity is genuine. To my homies—Jihad, Chico Cruz, and Ratsky—thanks for proofreading when I needed you. It's all love! To my city, Fort Pierce—Without my experiences in them trenches, this material wouldn't be as gritty and cut-throat. Even though it's a lot of treachery and senseless killing, I put on for you kuz you made me!

Killa Kounty - Stand up!

Cowards die many times before their deaths / The valiant never taste of death but once.
— William Shakespeare

Khufu

Chapter One

Suspended Animation

It was a late gloomy night at the run-down laundromat on 25th Street. Gloria had just put her last load of clothes in the washer and stepped outside to smoke a Virginia Slim. She took extended drags from the skinny cigarette and gazed at the interminable sky above her in adulation. From her observation of the stars and the moon, she concluded that there was an omnipotent force that man claimed to know about, but in all truth was inconceivable to the human mind. Noticing a falling star, Gloria wondered if her deceased lover was looking down at her. He was murdered a year ago in their home on her birthday, which was now a year-round remembrance of death.

At first, she was too terrified to testify, but constant pressure from Detective Archie and an identical resemblance of her lover in the face of her son changed that.

"I got'chu, baby," Gloria proclaimed out loud to herself, as she took another drag from her cigarette, then flicked it on the oil-stained parking lot. As soon as she walked back inside, the dryer made an annoying sound that made her know the clothes were done. Exhausted, she opened the dryer and began removing the clothes. Standing five feet flat, she had to stand on tiptoe to grab the garments from the large drier that sat against the tainted wall. Reaching to grab a pair of satin thongs, she felt the undeniable steel that was forcefully placed upon her cranium.

"Oh—my—God! Please—I have money in my car! You can—"*Boc!* All in one motion, the assailant put a hole in Gloria's head, caught her before she dropped, and stuffed her in the drier. After loading the drier with quarters, the victimizer unconcernedly left the premise, leaving Gloria tumbling in suspended animation.

Khufu

Chapter Two

Blood of his Father

"Come on, Nilya, pedal faster!" yelled Khafre as he pedaled ahead of her.

"I'm trying!" cried Nilya frightfully, as the pitbull growled at her back tire. Nilya was Shenida's daughter, who was a year older than Khafre—G's son. Shenida and Shantel had gotten close when G went in to face his murder charge. Shenida had convinced Shantel that she and G were only business partners, Desperate to get G home, Shantel would have befriended Donald Trump, if that's what it took. Shenida had come over to disclose the termination of the problem, which would soon get G home. She also brought new bicycles for Nilya and Khafre to ride while she talked with Shantel. Khafre and Nilya had decided to go looking for dogs to chase them, which Nilya was now regretting. Pedaling fast as she could, her foot slipped a pedal, sending her crashing to the jagged pavement. Nilya cried for help, while the red nose had a vicious clutch on her foot. Moments later, a brief sound that resembled screeching tires reverberated in the air. It was the sound of the pitbull shrieking after being stabbed through the top of its head. After killing the dog, Khafre continued to butcher the lifeless dog as if he were possessed.

"Protect what I love! Protect what I love! Protect what I love!" Khafre chanted the words of his father, until he was startled by a hand on his shoulder. Out of pure instinct, Khafre swung the knife around and pierced the flesh of the dog's owner.

"Sss—Ahh! You lil'fucka! You done killed my damn dog!"

"Come on, Khafre! Let's go," urged Nilya while hopping back on her bike. Khafre stood with knife in hand, never taking his eyes off the man whose dog he'd just mutilated.

"Where you stay at, lil' boy? I'm finna follow you home. Yo' parents gone have to buy me another, dog!"

"If you follow us, I'ma kill you!" declared Khafre, getting back on his bike and heading home. The man just stood there and watched the two kids ride away, believing every word that Khafre had stated. Before walking into the house, Nilya stopped Khafre and expressed her appreciation.

"Khafre, thank you for having my back. I was so scared," Nilya said.

"Nilya, you don't have to ever be afraid when you with me. I protect what I love," assured Khafre, pulling Nilya close and giving her a forehead kiss.

"Are you going to take your shirt off? It's so much blood on it," stressed Nilya.

"No, I don't hide anything from mama," Khafre stated before walking into the house. As soon as the kids walked into the house, the conversation between Shenida and Shantel came to an abrupt halt. Shantel rushed Khafre and lifted his shirt to see if he was wounded.

"Nilya, you okay?" asked Shenida, squatting to examine her daughter.

"Yes, mama. I'm fine."

"What happened, Khafre? Why are you covered in blood?" questioned Shantel.

"Mama, a dog tried to eat Nilya, so I killed it," Khafre calmly responded as if it wasn't his first kill.

"You said you killed it? How? Wit' what?" Khafre pulled the bloody knife from his pocket and held it by his side, while staring straight into his mother's eyes. Shantel glanced at Shenida, who gave off a look that seemed to say this was the start of a chaotic bloody path up ahead in Khafre's life.

"That boy got the blood of his father!" Shenida said matter-of-factly.

***

G was freshening up in his cell when he heard a female guard enter the dorm and began calling names for visitation.

"Moss! You have a visit!"

"Damn, that sounds like Kuz'o," G muttered, then rushed to finish brushing his teeth. G had a cousin named Shameka, who worked at the county jail. The first time G had ever made a trip to the county jail, his cousin, Shameka, would frequently make rounds to his dorm and check on him. She even flooded his account with some of that taxpayers' money she was getting. As time passed on and G's trips to the county jail became more common, Shameka started to disown him in front of her co-workers. G brushed the lent from his uniform and laughed at the irony of it all. *Hell—she is the one on the other side of the force. A fuckin' pig!*

"Moss, last call!" yelled the guard peevishly. Moments later, G strolled from his cell with the panache of a pimp and a gangsta, the whole time bearing a smirk on his face.

"How yo' doin' today, Shameka? My bad, excuse me—*Ms. Moss*, right?" asked G sarcastically.

"I see you still at it, huh?"

"Like a crack addict," replied G.

"I read what you did to your next-door neighbor. Boy, you is crazy as hell!"

"Don't concur wit' everything you read, kinfolks," G said in his defence as he pushed along, trying to reach the visitation room as quick as possible.

"Then the girlfriend of the man you killed just up and get killed a year later," said Shameka.

"Whoa!" said G, stepping in mid stride and locking eyes with his cousin. "First off, I'm appalled by these meritless and frivolous indictments!" said G in his best Ivy League impersonation. "Nay, I don't know what kind of westernized mind control them crackaz done indoctrinated you with, but you need to give yo' brain a bath! I refuse to let'chu fuck up my energy before my visit. Go, I'ma leave you wit' this—God helps those who helps themselves." G then proceeded to the sally port. All the dorms were glass, so G could see all inmates that were being held. He noticed a mortal enemy on the glass, grilling him like he wanted smoke.

"What it is? What it ain't, my nigga?" taunted G.

"Nigga, you know my work," the inmate, named Bean, replied on the other side of the glass.

"Weak azz nigga! You missed! That's not a kill, Mister Snitch!". When G was sixteen, Bean—who was the same age—had shot at G but missed. One day G spotted Bean purchasing some weed on the side of the store on 17th Street and Avenue D. G pulled his rusty .38 revolver and tried desperately to creep up on Bean, so that he could get a headshot, but Bean peeped him and ran for the fence. Just when Bean thought he had gotten away, G caught him on the fence and shot him in his ass, causing him to flip over the fence. Instead of pursuing him, G left him there. Bean pressed charges, but they were later dropped due to his recantation of statements and refusal to testify.

"Book a visit, police azz nigga! I'll beat yo' fuck azz in there!" threatened G. If Bean booked a visit, he would be placed in the same room with G. Something Bean definitely didn't want.

"See what I'm talking about? Leave that boy alone and come on!" Shameka stated, now agitated.

"Me and you forever, baby," G assured Bean before walking off. When G entered the visitation room, Shenida was already on the screen. She looked appealing as ever. G picked up the receiver and just gazed at Shenida in awe.

"What up, daddy? You okay?"

"Yea, I'm good. I'm just mesmerized. You lookin' good like a beauty queen! Damn, I miss you, ma."

"I miss you too, G-Baby. You won't be in here long. I threw a party for ole girl the other night. I got her wasted," stated Shenida, speaking in code about the murder she committed at the laundromat.

"Damn, I wish I was there. You know how much I love to party."

"You party a lil' too much, if you ask me. Listen, Shantel ain't gone be able to make the five-thirty visit. She had to work, so I brought yo' son wit' me.

"Khafre, here wit'chu?" asked G-Baby, surprised.

"Yea, he standing off to the side. I'ma put'em on the phone soon." For the next couple of minutes, Shenida gave G the rundown on how Khafre butchered a dog to protect Nilya, and the look in his eyes after he did it.

"Put my son on the phone." Shenida handed Khafre the phone and stood behind him.

"Hey, daddy," Khafre said calmly.

"What's goin' on, my lil' king? You know your name came from a king, right?

"I didn't know that, daddy."

"Well, now you do. Always remember, you're a king. you hear me?"

"I hear you, daddy. I'm a king."

"I heard about what you did for Nilya. I'm proud of you," said G.

"I just did what you told me to do, daddy."

"And what was that?"

"Protect what I love."

"That's right. But I also want'chu to remember to never love something or someone to the point where it makes you weak. You can love it, but don't be weak. You understand me?"

"Yes, daddy, I understand you."

"A'ight, good. You already know daddy loves you."

"I love you too, daddy," said Khafre, holding back tears, refusing to let his father see him cry.

"What are you?"

"I'm a king."

"Put Shenida back on the phone."

"What's good, G?" asked Shenida.

"You already know. What's good at your end?"

"Everything's everything. I got'chu, daddy. It's anything for my nigga."

Back in the car, Shenida occasionally glanced at Khafre as he gazed out of the window in deep thought.

"Khafre, you okay?"

"Yes, ma'am, I'm okay. Can I ask you a question?"

"Yeah, Khafre. What's up?" Shenida inquired, eager to know what was on Khafre's mind.

"What are you to my daddy?" Khafre asked, turning to face Shenida, making direct eye contact.

17

"Me and your father are good friends. We do good stuff in partnership and make a lot of money together. He asked me to help your mother look after you."

"I'm the man of the house now that daddy's gone. I can take care of myself," Khafre stated, sounding absolute.

"That's right, you are the man of the house now, but if you need anything just call me. I'ma buy you a phone tomorrow, okay?"

"Yes, ma'am."

"So what'chu like to do? What'chu wanna be when you get older?"

"I wanna protect people."

"So you wanna be a police or something?"

"No, ma'am! The police took my daddy away from me. I wanna protect people from the police. I wanna be a police killer." Khafre sounded serious to the core..

"Oh, shit," Shenida whispered under her breath. "You sure you don't wanna be a bodyguard or a fireman?"

"No, ma'am. I wanna protect people like my daddy did me."

"Okay. We'll talk more about it later. Okay?"

"Yes, ma'am."

Chapter Three

Good News, Bad News

It was a little over one in the morning in Rock Road County Jail. The inmates were rowdy and full of energy from the coffee they purchased from the canteen earlier in the day. G sipped from his cup, as he listened to his cellie tell war stories on how he laid the murder game down. Jimmy and G were from the same turf, so he felt comfortable telling G anything whatsoever.

"Yeah, my nigga! I was tellin' fool, get da fuck off my block. I even gave a warning shot, but da nigga just stood there, and had da nerve to tell me, he don't see dat shit! Shid—I guess you know. Sent two up top. Before he even hit da ground, I'm like: *look at what'chu made me do, dumb nigga*! I spit on 'neem and kicked him in his azz, ya hear me? Dem crackaz caught my azz in Texas and beat my azz," laughed Jimmy, unbothered.

"You tripped out! My nigga, you hit dat man in front of every-body," explained G.

"Aye! It is what it is, my nigga," replied Jimmy.

"Moss! Moss, you up?" asked the guard through the intercom.

"Yeah, what up?" asked G-Baby, perplexed.

"Pack your stuff. You're out of here," announced the guard, popping G's cell.

"A'ight, I'm comin!"

"Damn, my nigga. You gone. Don't forget me when you get out there," stressed Jimmy.

"I got'cha, bra. Here, you want this shit?" asked G, dumping all his food on Jimmy's bunk.

"Nigga, you know I want dat shit! What kinda question is dat?" replied Jimmy, putting the food in his bin. G threw his mattress over the rail, then went back in the cell to say his farewell.

"Listen, my nigga. No matter what they came at'chu wit', keep it gangsta. We don't do tellin!"

"Don't disrespect me, fam! You know my pedigree," stated Jimmy.

"A'ight—I'm out," said G, hugging Jimmy before leaving. On the way to booking, all G could think about was his son.

"Moss! Step into that room and put these on," ordered a guard, handing G a blue uniform.

"What the fuck ya handin' me this shit for? Where my clothes at?" questioned G abrasively.

"Moss, I have some good news and some bad news. Which one you want first?"

"Good news."

"Your murder charge was dropped."

"Shid—dat's fuckin' great news! What could the bad news possibly be?"

"You've been indicted by the Feds."

***

"Moss, one-thirteen visit—let's go!" yelled the old military veteran dick head guard. *One-thirteen* was an attorney visit. It was impossible for G to get any sleep due to his sudden misfortune of being indicted. He'd been brought over to the federal holding side of the jail, a little after two a.m. Placed in a cell alone, the thought of why he had been indicted circled the periphery of G's consciousness and parked in his forebrain.

"Moss! Where you at? Let's go!" yelled the guard.

"I'm right here, man—damn! Aint'chu still on da clock? You gettin' paid to do nothin—relax!" said G.

"Moss, I see this has become a revolving door for you. You're in the big league now. Federal!" stated Officer Perkins.

"Aye, man. It is what it's gone be," replied G. Officer Perkins made small talk, and told tasteless jokes on the tedious walk to one-thirteen, but G couldn't even hear him. He had zoned out to another realm as anxiety enveloped him. G had heard all the horrid stories about how dirty the Feds play, and was now about to experience it first-hand. They entered the sally port where an officer was checking inmates in.

"Officer Perkins! Who you got with you?"

"This here is the one and only notable *Mr. Moss!*" proclaimed officer Perkins sardonically.

"The notable Mr. Moss, huh?" remarked the check-in officer in a strong southern redneck drawl. "Okay then, there, Mr. Notable. Your attorney is already here, in *room one.*" On the way to their room, G saw a few of his homies that had been hidden by the system for years. He acknowledged them and kept it pushing. G entered the room, and had a seat across from his attorney, who looked as if he had years of experience practicing law. He looked Italian and appeared to be in his late forties.

"Mr. Moss! I'm your attorney, Mr. Peacock. How you feelin'?"

"I'm livin'. What up, though? Da fuck da Feds want wit' me?"

"Well, looks like you been indicted on a 922, G."

"Da fuck is that?"

"It's a firearms charge. The firearm that they recovered from your home was not manufactured in the state of Florida, so you're being charged as if you personally trafficked that firearm across state lines."

"What firearm? They never caught me wit' a gun!"

"Says here they recovered one from your home. They were going to arrest the mother of your child, but she told them she knew nothing about a firearm in the house." G thought long and hard then suddenly remembered that he had bought a pearl handled 357 magnum from Pony Boy. He was going to gift it to Shenida but left it in his shoe box. Then he remembered wiping it down before putting it away.

"That was a whole year ago! How can they charge me wit' a gun they found a year ago?"

"It's the Feds, man. They do what they want."

"Fuck it! I know for a fact it ain't no prints on it. Tell dem crackaz I said, *run it!*"

"Well, hold on. You got a bond hearing on Thursday. Let's see how that goes, then we'll go from there," pronounced Peacock.

"You think I can get a bond?"

"It'll be a long shot, considering your record, but we'll try," replied Peacock, straightening his tie.

"I got two felonies. My record ain't fucked up."

"Like I said, we'll see on Thursday. Is there anything you want to ask me or tell me before you leave?"

"Nah. I'ma see you Thursday," replied G as he got up to leave.

"Moss!"

"Yeah?"

"Don't talk about your case to anyone and watch what you say on the phone."

"I gotta gun charge, not a hunid kilo conspiracy. I think I'm pretty safe."

"Trust me, you're in the Feds now. It's a whole different level of snitching going on. Now I don't mean to be stereotypical but from the looks of you, I'm sure you've done some insidious shit in your life. So, don't go back there with your homies and tell war stories. Just stay to yourself."

"Anything else, Doctor Strange?" joked G. Peacock laughed.

"No, Moss. See you Thursday."

***

Later that day, Shenida was riding around and gettin' it, picking up money that was owed. Normally, she wouldn't front work out, but after years of dealing with the same people, she decided to give it a try. She wanted to see if they would bite the hand that fed them. Hopping out of her new Benz truck, Shenida pranced up to pink lip Joe's door and knocked aggressively. Moments later, the door swung open and one of Joe's hoodrats stood in the doorway.

"Bitch! What da fuck wrong wit'chu, knockin' on my door like you crazy or something?"

"I got'chu, bitch, right here," announced Shenida, pulling a compact 9mm from her Channel hoodie, and sticking it in the hood-rat's face.

"Ooowww! I am so sorry! Please don't shoot me!"

"Shut da fuck up, hoe! Where Joe at?" asked Shenida, her voice ringing with indignation.

"He on the side of the buildin' gamblin'."

"The next time I come through dis mothafuka, hoe, you better show pure humility or I'ma give yo' ugly azz a lobotomy!" threatened Shenida.

"A lo who?"

"Shut da door before I kill yo' dumb azz!"

The hoodrat closed the door and locked it. Chain included. When Shenida made it around the building, Joe was squatting with his back turned to her, rolling dice.

"Yeah, all you niggaz gettin' put out tonight, kuz I'm sendin' dat azz home broke!" yelled Joe, rolling a seven on the come out.

"Shid! I ain't gettin' put out of nowhere! I own my house! Fuck is you talkin' 'bout, pussy pink lip azz nigga!" replied an old head from around the way.

Crack! Shenida hit Joe in the back of his head, dropping him and pointing her pistol at the two old heads who were with him.

"Lie down on ya stomachs hands out, last time tellin' you!" The old heads did as they were told without a sound. While Joe rolled around on the ground holding his head, Shenida went through the old heads' pockets, then picked the money from the dice game up. She then stood over Joe, looking murderous.

"Where dat paper at, Joe?" Shenida asked through clenched teeth.

"Shenida? Man, you trippin'! Da fuck you hit me for?" cried Joe.

"You got my money?"

"Yea, come through tomorrow. I'll have it!" retorted Joe, still holding his head.

"I got a daughter to feed today! Fuck tomorrow! Go get my shit!" demanded Shenida.

"Man, just give me—" *Boc! Boc! Boc!* Shenida let off three shots on the side of Joe's head, nearly inducing a heart attack in the chest of the old heads. Joe grabbed at his head to see if any pieces were missing.

"Man, give dat hoe her money before she kill all our asses out here, silly nigga!" advised one of the old heads.

"A'ight! A'ight! Shit! I'm finna go get it now!" cried Joe

"Get'cha azz up and go get my shit," demanded Shenida, snatching Joe up by his shirt and kicking him in his ass. "Hurry the fuck up, nigga!" yelled Shenida, heading to her truck. *I can't believe this nigga almost made me kill 'em*, thought Shenida. As soon as she got in her truck, her phone rang.

"Hello! You have a prepaid call from the county jail from inmate "G". Press 5 to accept." Shenida accepted the call.

"Baby girl, what's up wit' it?" asked G.

"I'm just movin' around a lit bit. Another day in the field. You know how that shit go. How you? You good?" "Always! Listen, drop two bands in Jimmy Reeves' account for me."

"Say none. You need somethin'?"

"Not right now. How my son doin'?"

"He good. I bought him a phone, so you can call him whenever."

"Dat's what's up. Just so you know, them people dropped that murder charge."

"Yeah? I'm finna come get'chu. Shid! I want that dick first!" Pink lip Joe tapped on Shenida's window.

"Hold on, daddy." When Shenida let down her window, Joe handed her forty-two thousand dollars.

"It ain't gotta be all dat, Shenida baby. I just—" Shenida pointed her gun in Joe's face, cutting his words short. Joe backed away with his hands up, while Shenida let her window back up and pulled off.

"My bad, G. I'm on my way to get'chu, boo."

"You can't come get me, ma. They not lettin' me go."

"Why not?" questioned Shenida, confused.

"The state dropped the murder charge, but the Feds indicted me on a gun charge. They found that gun a year ago in my house. This shit wild!"

"Damn, daddy! How you get caught lackin' like that? Ain't no hardware suppose' to be over that way. What they talkin' 'bout?"

"I gotta bond hearing Thursday. I'ma see what I'm facing then."

"Whatever the bond is, daddy, you know you good!"

"I been askin' around. Niggas is sayin' the only way to get a bond is if you tellin' some shit. If that's the case, I ain't going nowhere."

"Whatever happens, daddy, I'm wit'chu. I love you, nigga!"

"Love you too, ma."

"You told Shantel yet?"

"Nah. I'ma wait till after bond hearing. I wanna see what I'm facing first. I don't want nobody there. Not even you."

"Nigga, you got me fucked up! Let dem crackaz get to talkin' crazy. I'ma go Jonathan Jackson on their fuck ass!"

"What'chu know 'bout Jonathan Jackson?" asked G, surprised.

"Nigga, I'on just fuck good. I slang pistols as well! I'ma profoundly intellectual prolific type bitch! Don't sleep on my skills!"

G laughed wildly, drawing attention from a few inmates.

"It's nice to hear you laugh in the face of adversity. You a real one."

"You ain't tellin' me nothin' I'on know. I'ma call you later. I ain't get no fuckin' sleep last night. I thought them folks had done book me on one."

"Well, just hit me when you get up. I'm finna come drop the money in Jimmy account then take it in. Love you, daddy."

"Love you too." *Click!*

Khufu

Chapter Four

Shut The Hell Up!

Khafre, now in the fifth grade, sat in class in a vexed state of mind, as his teacher rambled about blacks being slaves and criminals. Ever since his father had told him that he was a king, he'd been researching on the internet with the phone that Shenida had bought him. Khafre was intrigued with some videos he stumbled across titled *Hidden Colors*—one through five. Even at age eleven he was able to comprehend the information the black scholars were dropping. As soon as he was about to raise his hand and rectify her inaccuracy on black history, his phone rang.

"Hello?" answered Khafre.

"You have a prepaid call from G. To accept, press five, To decline, press—"

"What's up, pops?" asked Khafre.

"Khafre! Hang that phone up! Talking on your phone in my classroom is beyond unacceptable!" yelled Khafre's teacher—Ms. Cramtree.

"Pops, I gotta go. My teacher acting crazy about me being on the phone."

"Okay, I'll call you later on. I just wanted to hear your voice and let'chu hear mine. I love you, son."

"Love you too, pop." *Click!*

"Khafre! I will not put up with such behavior in my classroom!"

"Man, shut the hell up!" said Khafre as his jaw tensed.

"I beg your pardon?" retorted Ms. Cramtree.

"You heard me! You standing up there making it seem as if blacks were always slaves. Tell the truth! White people were some of the first slaves ever! Black people created math, science, medicine and astrology. We taught the world everything and we still are. Without black people the world would be boring. Y'all need us."

"It seems to me that you're living in a fantasy world," stated Ms. Cramtree.

"The first eighteen dynasties were black! That means the pyramids were built long before white people came from the caves of Europe," said Khafre, smirking.

"Aliens built the pyramids. Blacks had no such knowledge!"

"You ever seen an alien, Ms. Cramtree?"

"Out of my classroom now! Head straight to the principal's office!" ordered Ms. Cramtree. Khafre grabbed his backpack and headed towards the door while his classmates gazed at him in confusion and adulation. They had no idea what Khafre was speaking so assuringly about, but Ms. Cramtree did.

"Ms. Cramtree, I know that the truth can be scary and frightening, but I want you to know that you don't have to fear me. I'm your historial father," said Khafre, pushing the button to the front office before leaving the class. Moments later, administration spoke through the intercom.

"Ms. Cramtree! Is everything okay?"

"Umm—it is now. I have a student on the way to you now. Khafre Moss."

"Okay. We'll take care of it."

"Thank you," said Ms. Cramtree, taking a seat at her desk. "Everybody, back to work!" demanded Ms. Cramtree.

"You didn't give us an assignment yet," replied a freckled face redhead named Pete.

"Just write in your journals about your night last night!" ordered Ms. Cramtree as she rocked back and forth in a swiveled chair, confounded as to how a fifth grader could retain such complex information. A black kid at that.

***

Khafre had already called his mother on the way to the principal's office and told her to come and get him. Shantel was exasperated about having to leave her job and had it in mind to vent her feelings to him.

"Come in and have a seat," said Dr. Washington, who was the principal of Manatee Elementary.

"Moss, you mind telling me what happen between you and Ms. Cramtree?"

"No, I don't mind, Dr. Washington. First, how you doing today?"

"I'm fine, Moss, how about yourself?"

"I'm actually feeling pretty good today," admitted Khafre.

"That's nice to know, Moss. Now go ahead and tell me what happened."

"Well, Ms. Cramtree was making it seem as if black people were just slaves and criminals. I kindly informed her that white people were some of the first slaves, and that blacks created math, science and astrology. I didn't disrespect her." Dr. Washington gazed at Khafre with a deep reverence before speaking.

"I see that you are ahead of your time. Who taught you that?"

"My father. I also research on my own, sir."

"Well, as a black man myself, I must tell you that you are correct. But this is not the place for that kind of talk. Talking like that scares white people and when white people get scared they react irrationally or foolishly. You understand what I'm telling you?"

"Yes, sir."

"The school year is almost out. Just contain yourself and you'll be in sixth grade next year away from Ms. Cramtree. You think you can do that?"

"Yes, sir, I can do that."

"Okay. Keep researching, though. You're on the right track. I'ma look out for you until the school year is out."

"Yes, sir."

"Dr. Washington, Khafre's mother is here to pick him up," said the secretary.

"Okay—send her in," stated Dr. Washington. Moments later, Shantel entered the office, greeted Dr. Washington then had a seat next to Khafre. She glanced at her son who bared a carefree expression then turned her attention back to Dr. Washington. For the next fifteen minutes, Dr. Washington illustrated the compelling account between Khafre and Ms. Cramtree. He assured her that Khafre wasn't in any trouble and could return to school the following day.

On the ride home, Shantel was still in shock about her eleven-year-old son debating historical facts with his teacher. Considering the true situation now, she couldn't be mad at Khafre. She was more disappointed with herself for being thirty-seven and not knowing the history of her ancestors.

"Khafre!"

"Yes, mama?"

"Who told you all that stuff that you was tellin' yo' teacher?"

"When I went to see my daddy, he told me that I have a name of a king. He told me that I was a king too. I researched on my phone and found out that Khafre was a king in Egypt during the fourth dynasty. He ruled after his uncle Khufu. Then I watched all the "Hidden Colors" video series."

"What's *Hidden Colors*?" asked Shantel, perplexed.

"Don't worry about it, mama. I'll show you later."

"Listen, Khafre, I'm proud of you and I'm glad you know your history. But do me a favor and stop arguing with your teacher. I can't keep leaving work to come get'chu."

"I hear you, mama. I won't do it again." Shantel's phone rang. *"Hello?" You have a prepaid call from G. To accept, press—"*

"Whats good, ma?" asked G.

"Hey, baby! I miss you so damn much, man," whined Shantel.

"I miss that ass too! Can you talk or you busy?"

"I answered the phone, didn't I?"

"Oh, okay! You know I ain't doin' no trippin'. As long as I get my cut. Shid! Pussy ain't free," joked G.

"Boy! You gonna kill yo'self if I gave this good stuff away," replied Shantel, laughing.

"What stuff, mama?" asked Khafre.

"Mind ya business, Khafre."

"What Khafre doin' wit'chu? I just talked to him a while ago. He was still in school."

"I had to go get 'em. Apparently, he was in a heavy dialogue with his teacher about black history and shit got real. According to his principal, he won the debate. His teacher got in her feelings and sent him to the front office."

"My son is a fuckin' prodigy! Put 'em on the phone," demanded G.

"Hey, pops!"

"How you doin', king?"

"I'm good, pops. How about you?"

"You already know yo' pops a king too! Listen, you ain't do nothin' wrong! Keep doin' you and always remember what I told you."

"I'll never forget anything you tell me. I love you, pops."

"That's my young king! I love you too. Now put'cha mama back on the phone."

"What's up, daddy?" asked Shantel.

"Listen, they dropped the murder charge, but the Feds indicted me on a gun charge. It's a gun they found in the house a year ago. The same gun you forgot to tell me they found!"

"They had you in custody! I figured they was gon' tell you."

"Well, it seems to me that you were correct on your assumptions. Genius!" asserted G sardonically.

"Don't pop slick wit' me," replied Shantel mildly.

"Put my son back on the phone."

"Catchin' a attitude wit' me is not gon' better yo' situation. Whether I told you about the gun or not, you was still gon' get indicted anyway," cried Shantel.

"You done yet?"

"What'chu mean?"

"I ain't tryin' to hear that shit! Put my son on the phone." After kissing the back of her teeth, Shantel handed Khafre the phone.

"What's up, pops?"

"Khafre! Listen, I might be gone a lil' longer than I expected. I'ma need you to man up and make sure you take care of yo' mama. You a young man now. Wit' that being said, don't never let a man disrespect you or yo' mama. The minute a man disrespect—you stop him in his tracks! You crush 'em!"

"I understand, pop. I got it. I promise."

"Okay, that's what I love to hear. If you need something and yo' mama act like she don't wanna get it, call Shenida. You hear me?"

"Yeah, pop, I'm listening."

"As for your history, keep searching for knowledge of self. You are a descendant of royalty. This phone finna hang up. I'ma vibe wit'chu later. I love you, son.

"Love you too, pops." *Click!*

Chapter Five

Arm Career Criminal

"Your Honor, Mr. Moss has a history that qualifies him for 924(e) ACCA. He's an armed career criminal, facing a mandatory minimal of fifteen to life! I recommend that bail be denied," stated the racist prosecutor.

"Fifteen to life! Man, y'all got the wrong case number! I just gotta gun charge. The fuck y'all takin' 'bout?" G's nostrils flared in anger as he spat out those words.

"Your Honor, may I have a moment with my client?" asked Peacock.

"I suggest you contain your client or I will see to it that he's punished to the fullest extent!" said the judge in a philippic tone.

"Thank you, Your Honor. Moss, calm down. This is just the bond hearing."

"Calm down? Did you hear what that craka just said?"

"Yes, I heard him, Moss. We'll deal with it accordingly but not now."

"I beat that body, so now they tryna hang me for the gun!" expressed G loudly.

"Whassup, daddy? Say the word and I'll set this bitch off!" stated Shenida, ready to unleash venom towards the injustice that was being demonstrated on the man that she loved unconditionally. G knew that if he gave the order, Shenida would go to her car and come back in guns blazing. He couldn't let her lose her life and leave her daughter to be raised by the streets. Retraining his urge to lash out, G turned to Shenida and shook his head by way of saying, *No.*

"I'm cool, go ahead," said G to his attorney.

"Your Honor, my client—Mr. Moss—is an admirable and affable civilian. He's a very active, prolific pillar of his community. He's just had a baby boy, and he's also the breadwinner of his household. Mr. Moss needs to be out of bond fighting this case and preparing to leave his family established if he by chance loses this case."

"I've already viewed Mr. Moss's lengthy record and made my decision."

"I gotta one page record with two felonies. Fuck is he talkin' bout?" interrupted G.

"He has a resisting arrest without violence which alerts me that you have a bit of a rebellious side. Also, you're facing a mandatory minimal of fifteen years. You're a flight risk. Bail is denied," stated the judge while banging his gavel aggressively.

"I'll be there to see you tomorrow," said Peacock as a federal officer grabbed G to be taken back to a cold ass holding cell.

"I love you, daddy! You already know I got'chu! It's anything for my nigga," screamed Shenida, her voice dripping with passion. G glanced back at Shenida with confusion in his eyes. He couldn't understand why they were trying to give him half of his life in prison for a gun. The only thing he thought about was his son.

***

Three weeks later, G's attorney showed up bright and early to update him on the status of his case. G sat across from Peacock, feeling hopeless as he took cognizance of the distressing news.

"Well, looks like they have you by the balls, kid," said Peacock.

"How you figure that? They ain't even get the gun off me."

"Yeah, but your prints came back conclusive. Even if your prints came back inconclusive, you would still be fucked. You're a convicted felon. You can't be around firearms. This is not the state, this is the Feds."

"A'ight, fuck it! Tell 'em I'll take five years right now."

"You can't negotiate with the Feds. They tell you what you're facing and it's *take the plea or go to trial*," explained Peacock.

"What's the plea?"

"Fifteen," replied Peacock apathetically.

"Fuck no! Tell 'em, *run it*! We going to trial."

"If you lose, you could get eighteen or life. Let's think about this for a sec."

"I'm thirty. Fifteen is a life sentence for me. I'ma suit up!"

"Think about your son, okay? Now, I know all about Fort Pierce or—as your generation call it—Killer Kounty. You do not want the same streets that consumed you to raise your son. As your attorney, I have to present the notion that if you wanted to help yourself, the Feds would be willing to play ball."

"Do this look like the face of a fuckin' rat? Do the energy discharging off my body give you the perception that I'ma fuckin' cheese eater?" asked G as his pulse could be seen beating in his temple.

"No disrespect, Moss, but I've seen a lot in my years of law practice."

"Don't trip! I'ma get a paid attorney. I'm good on you, man."

"Why spend all that money on a lawyer just to get the same plea deal or worst? You're facing a mandatory fifteen. You can't get under that unless you cooperate. If you wanna go to trial, I'll fight tooth and nail for you. But understand that I had to present that offer to you."

"Tell them pussy crackaz we goin' to war!"

"Okay, war it is," stated Peacock, re-adjusting his tie. Now that we got that out of the way, can I be honest?" asked Peacock.

"What up," questioned G.

"I fucking hate snitches!"

***

"Mr. Moss, did you wish to say anything before I impose sentence?"

"Nah, I'm good!"

"Alright. It's the judgement of the court that the defendant, Mr. Moss, is hereby committed to the custody of the Bureau of Prisons to be imprisoned for a term of a hundred and eighty months." After the judge handed down the sentence, G couldn't hear anything else that was being said. He had zoned out, thinking about his son.

"Any recommendations, Mr. Peacock?"

"Judge, we would ask that he be confined close to South Florida as quickly as possible," stated Peacock.

"I'll make that recommendation. Good luck, Mr. Moss," stated the judge as if G was headed off to college or was about to take an exam or some shit.

"Keep yo' head up, daddy!" yelled Shenida, snapping G out of the daze that he was in. Even though he was emotionally depleted, G refused to show any sign of defeat. Instead, he smiled at the judge and held his head high as he was led out of the courtroom. Peacock had arranged to see G after sentencing, so he was placed in a holding cell, until he was seen.

"Moss! How you feeling?" asked Peacock.

"About as fascinatin' as yesterday's fuckin' oatmeal! I just got sentenced to fifteen years! How the fuck you think I'm feelin'?"

"Don't worry yourself. I'm going to appeal it. If we lose an appeal, you should still be good."

"How the fuck?" retorted G, agitated.

"It's a gang of new laws being passed. You won't do the whole fifteen."

"So until then—I'm buried alive, huh?"

"You tough, right? Be strong for your kid, and stay out of trouble while you're in there."

"It's a lil' too late to practice docility, man."

"Don't be an asshole. I'll mail you the appeal brief when it's done," assured Peacock.

"Yeah. Whatever, man."

"Hey, um—was that the mother of your child out there?"

"Nah. Why?"

"She's out there going bat shit crazy about you." G managed to fix his face to smile.

"That's my lil' ride or die."

Chapter Six

They Gone Tell on You

Two years later, Khafre headed to his bus stop, taking in the symphony of God's creatures. It was still dark outside, so Khafre was on guard. A youngin' was killed over typical gang beef just two days ago at the same bus stop. Khafre refused to be victimized over illogical means. He would rather die defending himself. He looked over himself, checking his gold Cuban necklace with a diamond-studded Africa charm, a Cuban bracelet, and rings on every finger. Brushing off his Fendi sweat suit, a glare from a metallic object caught his attention out of his peripheral vision. Khafre picked the object up and saw that it was a .38 special. With no hesitation, he put the revolver in his Louis Vuitton backpack and ran to catch his bus that had just pulled up. As Khafre boarded the bus, he found it ironic how Rosa Parks stood her ground to sit in the front of the bus, but the first place that young blacks headed to was the back of the bus. Khafre's reason for doing so was simply to watch everything. Ever since Khafre saw the interview of Alpo on YouTube telling how he had Mitch killed, he had a phobia about letting people sit behind him.

"Hey, Khafre," greeted Toya in a seductive monotone. She had a crush on Khafre since the beginning of the school year. Toya wasn't Khafre's type, so he just kept it cordial with her.

"Toya, what up wit' it?" replied Khafre, taking a seat.

"How come you ain't accept me on Facebook yet?" whined Toya.

"Next time I log in, I got'cha," Khafre promised then put on a pair of Raycon earbuds and vibed out to a new female artist by the name of Mulatto. Forty-minutes later, now in Port St. Lucie, the bus was pulling into Southport Middle School. Khafre stepped off the bus last in his Fendi shoes and sweats. He'd been growing his hair for two years, and it was already shoulder-length. With a complexion similar to his mother's, Khafre looked like an Afro-China man with thick dreadlocks. Malice was thick in the air as Khafre swayed through campus, but the females loved him.

"Hey, big head!" said Nilya excitedly.

"What dey do, lil' head?" replied Khafre, hugging Nilya and kissing her on the cheek. Toya gave them both a look of incredulity, kissed her teeth and stormed off, wishing Nilya was her.

"I see your little girlfriend Toya living in her feelings right now about 'chu kissing me," joked Nilya.

"She'll be a'ight. I don't entertain sophomoric females."

"*Soft ma* who?" questioned Nilya.

"Immature. I don't entertain immature girls. I don't like females who wear weave and—or—face full of Maybelline make-up. I like my women all natural like you."

"Awweeee! I'm flattered," proclaimed Nilya as they headed inside the cafeteria.

"I'm serious, girl! You lookin' good in yo' lil' Chanel dress," complimented Khafre.

"Thank you. You don't look bad yourself."

"Don't look bad? Girl, I'm palatable wit' this shit," bragged Khafre.

"Boy, whatever!" stated Nilya, hitting Khafre on the arm playfully. After grabbing their breakfast, they sat, talked, and picked over their food for ten minutes.

"I'm done, Khafre, you finish?" asked Nilya.

"Yeah, we can go," assured Khafre, getting up to put his tray away, with Nilya right behind him. On the way out of the cafeteria, Khafre peeped four dudes who had been watching him and Nilya ever since they entered the cafeteria.

"Nilya, walk me to the restroom before we go to class."

"Okay. You better not make me late for homeroom, big head." Nilya waited outside while Khafre went in to use the restroom. Khafre headed straight to the middle stall, pulled the .38 from his backpack and had a seat on the toilet. Moments later, the four miscreants mobbed in the restroom in tandem, the last one speaking to Nilya.

"What's up, Nilya baby?" said K.D.—the aggressive one of the bunch.

"Boy! Whatever!" said Nilya, dismissing him. When K.D. entered the restroom, his comrades were posted in front of the stall that Khafre was in.

K.D. yelled: "Come on outta there, my boy! You know what it is!" When Khafre didn't respond, K.D. kicked the door to the stall in and found himself staring down the barrel of a .38.

"What the fuck is up? Huh?" asked Khafre as calm as a surgeon.

"Shit! Oh—shit, man! I—," stuttered K.D. Khafre snatched K.D. by his collar and cracked him across his nose, breaking it instantly. The other three ran out of the bathroom as if Khafre was pulling off the pin from some grenade. Startled and confused, Nilya entered the restroom and found Khafre standing over K.D., inflicting crucial punishment.

"Oh my God! Khafre—stop! Stop it! You gon' kill 'em!" exclaimed Nilya, grabbing Khafre's shirt. Khafre turned to swing behind him but saw that it was Nilya and stopped mid swing. When Khafre turned around, K.D. was stumbling out of the restroom, wailing in agony.

"Khafre, they gon' tell on you! Give me the gun, hurry up!" demanded Nilya, snatching the gun from Khafre, and putting it in her Chanel bag. Come get it after school," said Nilya, storming out of the restroom. Khafre washed and dried his hands. When he walked outside, he was swarmed by deans and the resource officer.

"I'm going to have to ask you to lie on the ground and put your hands behind your back," stated the resource officer.

"Man, you see what I got on? I'll put my hands behind my back, but I ain't laying on no ground," said Khafre as he turned around and put his hands behind his back. The officer moved in, detained Khafre and took him to the front office. After being searched by damn near the whole administration, Khafre was made to have a seat.

"Moss, what did you do with the gun? And before you lie to me, I want you to think about something. We have four people saying they saw you with it. One of them has a broken nose, and a fractured clavicle. Again, if you lie to me, I'm going to allow this officer to take you to jail. Understand?" asked Principal Snail.

"Yes, sir. I understand what you're saying fully. However, I don't know why you guys were told that I had a gun. Why would I bring a gun to school? That would be imprudent."

"*M*, who?" asked Principal Snail, perplexed and amazed.

"*Foolish*! That would have been foolish of me, Principal Snail. I simply went in to use the restroom and in walks these guys demanding that I fork over my jewelry. I merely defended myself. No gun. I don't mean to be brash or boastful, but—Principal Snail—my knuckle game is nice," assured Khafre, drawing laughter from Principal Snail and the resource officer.

"Moss, you seem to be quite different from the kids your age. You have potential to be something great. I tell you what we're going to do—a thorough search of the restroom. If we don't find anything, I'll let you go home, but you'll be suspended for ten days."

"Fine with me, boss," replied Khafre.

Chapter Seven

We Gotta Talk

Fifteen months earlier, G was transferred from Miami's federal facility to Coleman USP. When G hit the pound, there were inmates from all over the world hugging the fence and trying to see what new homies they had. A lot of inmates who got off the bus with G were "*hot*"—prison slang for a snitch—but thanks to emails, majority of the shot callers already knew who was telling. They were marked men, and didn't even know it.

"Aye, homie! Where you from?" asked an inmate named Paul.

"I'm from Florida."

"What part of Florida?"

"I'm from Fort Pierce," G replied arrogantly.

"Oh, you from Killa Kounty, huh?"

"Already."

"Alright, homie. It's a few of y'all on the pound. The homies from Florida sit over there on them bleachers. Go, put'cha stuff up and come meet the homies. My name Paul, but they call me P. Moe. I'm from Palm Beach."

"A'ight. They call me G."

"Okay, G. I'ma let the homies know you here. What block you in?"

"They put me in A-Block."

"I'm in A-block too. We gon' chop it up."

"Already!" stated G, walking off, heading to his living quarters. When G entered A-block, he had to go through a metal detector before he could fully enter the block. Once G was in, he saw niggas shooting dice, playing poker, talking shit over chess games and selling everything from liquor to fried chicken. *Damn, this shit just like the streets*, thought G.

"What's up, young blood?" asked Hunt. Hunt was a kingpin from West Palm Beach.

"What up wit' it?" G replied.

"You come in with a boat load of it too?" questioned Hunt.

"What'chu mean?" asked G, confused.

"Time."

"Oh, hell yeah! Them crackaz gave me fifteen."

"Ahh—Shid! That ain't no time. I got twenty-one life sentences. I done did yo' time already," boasted Hunt.

"Damn!"

"Yeah, man. Them hot azz niggaz told on me. What room you in?"

"One-ten."

"You gotta good cellie. You in there with A. He from Pompano. Go ahead and get situated. I'll rap wit'chu later," assured Hunt, turning his MP3 back on and walking off to go finish his workout. When G got to room one-ten, he knocked then walked in.

"What's good, bra? I'm—" G's words were cut short when he saw who his cellie was.

"G?"

"Mothafuckin', Aaron? Man, this shit crazy! Nigga, I was blowin' yo' phone up until Mango told me you was facin' a few bodies."

"Yeah, crackaz had me jammed up. I beat all them shits, though."

"So, what they charged you wit'?" asked G.

"Crackaz gave me fourteen for conspiracy. I heard 'bout Mango. That's fucked up."

"Yeah, It's all good though!" G stated, letting Aaron know that he avenged his homie's death.

"The fuck them crackaz got'chu on?" questioned Aaron.

"The state had me on a body, but I beat it. They found a gun in my house. The Feds picked that shit up and charged me wit' it a year later. They nailed me and gave me fifteen."

"Damn! Them crackaz ain't playin' 'bout them guns. Listen, you can't go to the store until next week. I'ma put'chu a care package together, to get'chu through."

"Nah, I'm good. I'll wait till we get to the store."

"How the hell you gon' brush ya teeth and shower wit'no soap? Stop all that pride shit, man. I got'cha," Aaron said reassuringly.

Moments later, an old head named Todd—from Fort Lauderdale Florida—walked in the room, with some turkey wraps.

"What's up, A? Who this? The new homie?" asked Todd.

"Yeah, this G. He from Fort Pierce," said Aaron, grabbing a wrap.

"Fort Pierce? Them niggas down there been killin' since the sixties."

"Already!" confirmed G.

"Already, huh? You got'cha paper work already?" asked Todd.

"I got my PSI," replied G, referring to his pre-sentencing information.

"That's cool or whatever, but the homies gon' wanna see them sentencing transcripts."

"I ain't gotta problem showin' my paperwork. I'm official! But them niggas gone have to show me they shit too," proclaimed G.

"I already seen all the homies' paperwork. They straight. But if that's what'chu want, I can arrange that," assured Todd, removing a small notepad and pen from his back pocket.

"Yeah. That's what I want," said G-Baby.

"A'ight. Give me ya information." After G gave Todd his info, Todd left to go drop it in the mail.

"Damn, my nigga. Calm down. This how this shit go," said Aaron.

"I really like—low-key feel disrespected," admitted G.

"My nigga, I know yo' paperwork straight! You a solid nigga but this process everybody gotta go through. Bitch, you trippin! Let's go outside, so you can meet the homies," stated Aaron, stepping out of the room with G behind him. Once outside, Aaron continued to school G on how shit operated in the pen.

"You know you gone have to get'chu a knife, right?"

"Shid, make it happen," replied G.

"You know I got'cha, bih," assured Aaron. *Boom!* G got low like a shell-shocked veteran. Aaron laughed as he took a squat on the ground.

"What the fuck was that?"

"That's a bomb them crackaz be throwing out of that tower over there when some shit jump off. See them AB's over there, fuckin' that other craka up?"

"Yeah."

"They got word through email that he was hot. Everytime a bus come, somebody get fucked up or die."

"Damn, shit real," said G.

"Oh yeah, bih, we got tension wit' them Carolina niggaz, so be on point.

"Damn, nigga, I just got here."

"Welcome to the pin, bih," replied Aaron, smiling.

Chapter Eight

What Happen to You?

Shantel wasn't angry that Khafre had gotten suspended for defending himself. She was more vexed that he wore all of his jewelry to school, enticing the have-nots.

"Khafre! Why the hell would you wear all that jewelry to school?" asked Shantel.

"Because, mama, I'ma descendant of royalty! A king should alwayz present himself as such," declared Khafre.

"Oh gawd! I'ma have to tell Shenida to stop buying you all that stuff."

"Come on, mama. Don't hate on my lil' drip."

"Just mind how you flaunt your jewelry!"

"Stop right here, ma! Stop!" Shantel brought her Lexus truck to an abrupt halt.

"Boy! What the hell wrong wit'chu?"questioned Shantel.

"Nothing, ma."

"Anyways, you got'cha house key?"

"Yeah, ma, I got it."

"Okay. I'm goin' back to work. Tell Nilya I said hi."

"A'ight ma," muttered Khafre, hopping out of the truck and heading towards the park on Avenue M to wait for Nilya. In front of the park, there were three-feet logs lodged into the ground vertically four feet apart. Khafre was standing on one of the logs when Nilya's bus pulled up. Just the sight of her bus made Khafre replay the altercation that took place in school. He was amazed at how Nilya had rushed herself to save him. The thought of it made Khafre smile. Nilya was the last one to get off the bus. Her hair was in disarray, and the front of her Channel dress was torn, showing her matching lace bra. As the bus pulled off, Khafre approached Nilya.

"What the hell happened to you?"

"Boy, nothin! I'm a'ight," lied Nilya.

"Lie to me again!"

Nilya sucked her teeth before answering.

"Them hatin' azz hoez jumped me on the bus."

"What hoez?"

"Them two hoez walkin' right there."

Khafre went in Nilya's Chanel bag and grabbed his .38.

"Come on!" yelled Khafre, grabbing Nilya by the hand, forcing her to run with him. Once in striking distance, Nilya grabbed Tee Tee by her sew-in weave and pulled her to the ground, nearly snapping her neck. Nilya then wrapped her left hand in Tee's Tee's weave and hit her repeatedly with her right, drawing blood and causing lacerations.

"Get her! Somebody get her please!" cried Tee Tee. Saudia, who was Tee Tee's friend, tried to assist but was snatched up by Khafre. He put Saudia's face in the dirt and pushed his .38 aggressively in the back of her head.

"If you ever put yo' hands on Nilya again, I'ma kill you and yo' friend! You hear me?" asked Khafre, lifting Saudia's face out of the dirt.

"Yeah! Yeah! I hear you. Please!" cried Saudia.

"Aye, nigga! Get the fuck off my sister!" yelled Kurt. As soon as Khafre let Saudia up, she took off running full speed. Kurt saw the .38 in Khafre's hand but still took a swing at him. Khafre slipped the punch and hit Kurt with the .38, opening a cut above his left eye, dropping him to the ground. Khafre then straddled Kurt and went to work—pistol-whipping him vigorously. Moments later, the sound of screeching tires pierced the air waves.

"Nilya! Khafre! That's enough! Let's go!" announced Shenida who was late picking up Nilya.

"You know where I stay, hatin' azz hoe," Nilya whispered in Tee Tee's ear, then kicked her in the face before walking off. Khafre continued to beat Kurt senseless.

"I said, let's go! Khafre, now!" Khafre looked back at Shenida, then stood up.

"I'ma see you again, homie," Khafre proclaimed, kicking and spitting on Kurt before walking off. Once in the truck, Shenida pulled off, staring at Nilya, waiting on an explanation.

"Nilya, what the hell was that?"

"Them hoes were just hatin', ma."

"Hatin' on what?" asked Shenida with raised eyebrows.

"Kuz, mama, I be designer down, plus I look like Lora Harvey witta fatter fatty."

"Girl, whateva!" dismissed Shenida.

"Nah. But—farreal, mama—them girls jumped me. They said I think I'm all that,"

"You okay?"

"Yeah, mama, I'm good," assured Nilya, attempting to fix her weave.

"Khafre!"

"What up, G-ma?"

"Where the hell you get that gun from?"

"I found it."

"Give it here," demanded Shenida. When Khafre handed the gun to Shenida, she noticed that the skin and meat from Kurt's head was lodged in the side of the gun.

"G-ma, dude acted like he ain't like what was goin' on wit' his sister. I had to demonstrate. You know I'on play bout Nilya," said Khafre.

"After I drop Nilya home, we gotta have a talk."

"Yes, ma'am," replied Khafre.

The night was lustrous, the moon was full and the sky seemed to be decorated with every star born. Police sirens reverberated in the distance as fiends interacted with dealers up and down 9th Street. Khafre took it all in while Shenida smoked a blunt and schooled him. After seeing Khafre pistol whipping Kurt in the street, she had to bring him under her tutelage.

"Khafre, I understand you was just protecting Nilya and that's what'chu suppose' to do. But you pulled a gun on a man in front of everybody. Mothafukaz will tell on you, baby. Never pull a gun unless you gon' use it."

"I did use it, G-ma," replied Khafre.

"Yeah, but you let him live and on top of that, you dogged him out in the streets in front of everybody. You know what pride is?" asked Shenida.

"Yes, ma'am."

"Okay, so you know pride will make a man muder some shit. So, now you gotta get him before he get'chu. Is you ready for that type of shit?" Shenida asked, already knowing the answer.

"Yes, ma'am."

"*Yes, ma'am*, what?" questioned Shenida, looking Khafre in his eyes.

"Yes, ma'am, I'm ready to kill.

***

Pink lip Joe was sitting in the bootleggers' spot, bagging up molly. Anyone that came after hours to buy liquor, Joe would sell them molly along with their purchase. Fred was an old head who ran the bootlegger spot on 9th Street. He talked cold shit to Joe as he periodically took swigs from a Wild Irish Rose bottle.

"Awwl! Pussy pink lip ass nigga! You ain't worth the air you breathing, po' azz nigga!" said Fred.

"Old head, you washed up! I'm the new wave!" boasted Joe.

"New wave? Nigga, you pushin' forty! You ain't young no more, silly nigga!"

"I'm young enough."

"Yeah, okay. Go carry ya ass out there in them streets playin' wit' them young niggas then. They gon' fuck around and pop a hole in yo' dumb ass!"

"I'm in the streets! Fuck is you talkin' bout, old head? Them young niggas ain't gon' do shit to Joe."

"Okay, tough ass nigga!" replied Fred, taking another sip from his wine bottle. A sudden knock at the door startled Joe, causing him to tense up.

"What'chu jumpin' for, scary ass nigga?" said Fred.

"You got me fucked up. I'm a gangsta!" said Joe, trying to appear tough.

"Yeah, I hear you," laughed Fred all the way to the front door. Fred opened the door. To his surprise, it was a beautiful young woman.

"How you doin', baby girl? What'chu need?" asked Fred.

"You gotta bottle of gin?"

"Yeah I got'cha, come on in." The octave in the young woman's voice sounded familiar to Joe, causing him to look up from the table. The sight of Shenida caused Joe's heart to accelerate. His body tensed up as he became fidgety, trying to cuff the molly. Shenida made as if she didn't even notice Joe and continued to converse with Fred. All of a sudden Joe bolted for the back door and ran outside.

"What the hell wrong wit' that nigga?" asked Fred, turning to go check on Joe.

Boc! Shenida hit Fred in the back of his head, dropping him next to a case of Natural Ice beer. Joe continued to run in the field that was behind the house, never looking behind him. *Boc! Boc! Boc! Boc! Boc!* Khafre put five shots in Joe's back, dropping him by a sugar cane tree. Khafre jogged up to Joe's body, stood over him and put the last shot into Joe's enormous head. He then ran back to Shenida's truck where she awaited. Once in the truck, Khafre said nothing. He just sat back in his seat and gazed out of the windshield in a tranquil-like trance.

"You okay?" asked Shenida.

"Yes, ma'am."

"He dead?"

"Yes, ma'am."

"How ya know?"

"Kuz I hit 'em in his head," assured Khafre.

"Okay, good. You remember why he had to die?"

"He stole from you and my daddy."

"Right. So, how you feelin'?"

"Alive."

"As you should," said Shenida, putting the car in gear and pulling off. Oh the ride home Shenida could hear G in her head asking her to look after Khafre, and here it was. She'd just turned him to a killer. The thought of regret came and went as she evaluated in her mind that she was teaching Khafre how to survive in a cesspool full of killers. Pulling up in front of her home, Shenida killed the engine and removed the keys.

"Listen. What took place tonight can never be discussed, under-stand?"

"I'm on point, G-ma," proclaimed Khafre.

"I'm serious, don't even tell Nilya."

"I hear you, G-ma."

"Okay. I already told yo' mama that you spending the night over here. When we get in here, go in the hallway closet. I got'chu some clothes and shoes in there. Take a shower and leave them dirty ones in the bathroom. I'll get 'em when you finish.

"Yes, ma'am. G-ma, thank you."

"For what?" asked Shenida.

"Bringin' that beast outta me. I needed that for what I got planned."

"What'chu got planned?"

"I'll tell you later, G-ma. I'm tired."

"A'ight. Give me that gun before you go inside." Khafre handed Shenida the .38 then attempted to exit the truck.

"Khafre, hold up."

"What's up, G-ma?"

"Anytime, you need me for anything, I'm here."

"I know, God-mama. That's why I love you." Shenida rubbed her hand through Khafre's dreadlocks then pulled him close, giving him a forehead kiss.

"I love you too, baby."

The pressure from the shower head stimulated Khafre's scalp as he stood under the steamy hot water in deep thought. He won-dered what his father would think of him taking a man's life. Did the end justify the means? Khafre's thoughts were interrupted by someone entering the bathroom.

"Aye, who that?" asked Khafre.

"What'chu doin' over here, big head?" teased Nilya.

"What'chu doin' still up this time of mornin', lil' head? Don't chu got school tomorrow?" replied Khafre.

"I been up playin' candy crush. So where did you and my mama go?" questioned Nilya.

"We just rolled around and kicked it. Nothin' much," lied Khafre.

"So when we started lying to each other, Khafre?"

"No lies, Nilya."

"Then why you got blood on yo' shoes? Huh?"

Khafre hesitated before responding.

"That's from earlier when I stomped that nigga Kurt."

"You kicked him one time, Khafre. It's blood on both of yo' shoes, like it been sprayed on there. You know what? Never mind. It's fine you don't wanna tell me." Nilya made a dramatic exit from the bathroom. Khafre stood under the shower for ten more minutes then dried off and slipped into his Ferragamo pajamas and slide that Shenida had purchased for him. Khafre shifted through the hallway straight to Nilya's room. From the carpet to the ceiling, Nilya's room was garnished in Versace. Khafre often teased her about being a designer fiend. He entered her room and sat on the edge of the bed.

"Nilya, you mad at me?" Nilya ignored Khafre and continued to play candy crush. Khafre grabbed one of her feet and began to give her a foot massage.

"Hhh! Nilya exhaled and sucked her teeth. "Khafre, why is you lying to me? You suppose' to be like my best friend," whined Nilya.

"Nilya, you know you my heart. You know I never lied to you or kept anything from you, but on some real shit I'm asking you to leave this one alone. Just do that for me please," begged Khafre. Nilya knew in her heart that Khafre had done something atrocious, but decided to let it go.

"I guess I can let it go. You lucky you a good massager."

"That's not even a word, big head. It's *masseur*, genius," corrected Khafre.

"Like I said, a massager."

"You a whole trip no baggage,"

"Whatever, you love me though."

"You know it. Come here," demanded Khafre, leaning in, placing a kiss on Nilya's forehead. "Goodnight, big head," said Khafre, grabbing one of Nilya's Versace pillows before lying on the floor.

"You coulda slept up here wit' me. I wasn't gon' take nothin'," joked Nilya.

"Nah, I'm kool down here," Khafre stated, lying on the floor.

"A'ight then—goodnight, lil' head," said Nilya.

"Yea, yea," replied Khafre as he closed his eyes and replayed the moment he stood over pink lip Joe and took his life. Shenida was standing on the other side of the door, eavesdropping. She'd heard their entire conversation and was proud of how Khafre had handled himself. She walked away grinning in awe of her protégé.

Chapter Nine

You Played

Khafre awoke to the sounds of Nilya getting ready for school. He'd only managed to capture two hours of sleep due to anxiety. Catching his first body under the tutelage of his godmother had Khafre enthralled. He was now a killer like his father.

"Mornin', lil' head," muttered Nilya.

"Umm—what's up wit' it, scrub?" replied Khafre as he stretched.

"Gettin' ready to go to this bum ass school wit' hatin' ass hoes. I can't wait til' this year over. I'll be in high school next year away from their hatin' ass."

"You sound real crazy right now. There are hatin' hoes in high school too, big head."

"I'm just sayin'—"

"Saying what exactly?" asked Khafre.

"I'm just sayin', I gotta extra toothbrush in the bathroom. I suggest you got put it to use, kuz I know yo' breath foul like a dumpster full of garbage right now," Nilya said with a grin as she unwrapped a Versace scarf from around her head and started to put on all her jewelry. Khafre got up, snuck up on Nilya as she looked in the mirror, and kissed her repeatedly on her cheek.

"Uhhgg! Boy!" whined Nilya, wiping her face hysterically.

"Uhh—huh! Yeah!" taunted Khafre before going in Nilya's bathroom to brush his teeth. When Khafre departed from the bathroom, a delightful stench invaded his nostrils. He had never smoked before but knew immediately what the smell was that lingered in the air.

"Damn, you in here blowin'?" Khafre asked Nilya.

"Boy, you know I don't smoke. That's mama in there. She smoke every mornin'. I think she was callin' you too."

"Oh yeah? I'm finna go see what's up," replied Khafre, heading to the living room. Khafre made his way down the spacious hallway and found Shenida looking elegant in a Louis Vuitton robe. She subconsciously sat seductively with her legs crossed on an Armani sofa as she smoked a gravel leaf.

"Good mornin', God-mama. You called me?" asked Khafre as he admired Shenida's morning beauty.

"Mornin' to you too. Yea, I called you. How did you sleep?" questioned Shenida, blowing smoke out of her nose.

"I slept a'ight. What up, G-ma?"

"I'on feel like movin' right now. You mind walkin' Nilya to the bus stop?"

"You know I ain't got no problem wit' that, G-ma."

"Okay. Go look in my room on the bed. I got some clothes in there for ya. Leave them pajamas in there and put everything on that I sat out for you."

"Yes, ma'am. You look pretty this mornin' too, G-ma."

"Boy! Is you flirtin' wit' yo' God-mama?"

"No, ma'am, just complimentin' yo' mornin' beauty."

"Well, thank you. Now go get ready. It's almost time for Nilya to leave." Khafre did as he was told. When he inspected the clothes, Khafre saw that everything was Gucci down to the shoes, and next to the clothes was a cream colored SIG M17 9mm with a seventeen-round clip. As soon as Khafre laid eyes on it, it was love at first sight. He dressed quickly, tucked his new pistol, then B-lined towards Nilya's room.

"What's up, scrub? You ready?" asked Khafre.

"Where you goin', lookin all cute and stuff?"

"I'm walkin' you to the bus stop."

"Mama ain't takin' me to school?" asked Nilya.

"Nah. She asked me to walk you up. I'ma vibe wit'cha till yo' bus come."

"Okay. I'm ready, let's go," stated Nilya, grabbing her Versace bag.

"Nilya! You got money to eat wit'?" asked Shenida once Niya entered the livin' room.

"Yea, ma, I'm good. I love you. See you later," replied Nilya before walking out the door.

"Khafre, come back over here when Nilya get on the bus."

"Yes, ma'am," said Khafre then walked out behind Nilya. On the way to the bus stop, crickets and frogs seemed as if they were performing a duet. The ground was covered with mist and stray dogs ran the streets aimlessly.

"Khafre, I'm sorry 'bout last night. I ain't mean to aggravate you. I just wanted to know what was up."

"Don't sweat it. You good."

"You sure? You don't wanna talk about it?"

"Nah. We passed that. It's a new day."

"Okay. Whatever you say, lil' daddy. You coulda slept wit' me last night though. I was in my feelings 'bout that," admitted Nilya in a solemn tone.

"Come on, Nilya. If I wouda laid wit'cha, shit woulda went somewhere else."

"And?" replied Nilya, eyebrows raised.

"I ain't tryna fuck up our freindship, Nilya. I like what we got."

"Fuck up our friendship? Why you actin' like you some kinda experienced lover? Khafre you still a virgin like me."

"I know enough to know that sex changes shit."

"So, you want me to lose my virginity to somebody else and give away all this goodness?" asked Nilya with slight frown.

"First off, that's yo' stuff. Do you! And what make you think that stuff good?"

"Everybody know fresh ripen fruit is the tastiest. Full of flavor and shit. And boy—You'll lose yo' whole mind if I gave this stuff to somebody else," laughed Nilya.

"I'on care," replied Khafre, trying to sound convincing.

"Lies! Anyways—you coulda at least held me," exclaimed Nilya as her bus pulled up.

"Maybe next time, big head. See you when you get home." Khafre hugged Nilya.

"Bye, lil' head," replied Nilya before getting on the bus. After Nilya got on the bus, Khafre noticed that the bus stop wasn't as crowded as usual. Only three other people had gotten on the bus with Nilya. Khafre erased the thought from his mind and headed back to Shenida's. When he made a right on 29th and Avenue M, he noticed a group of girls making their way up the sidewalk behind him. He kept it moving and paid them no mind, until he heard their footsteps quicken.

"Uhh—huh! Yea, pussy ass nigga!" When Khafre turned around, he recognized Tee Tee and Saudia from the fight the day before at the bus stop. All together six girls had surrounded Khafre. The smallest one out of the bunch—Ranada—threw up her set as if to challenge Khafre.

"Man, y'all hoes betta find somebody to play wit'," advised Khafre.

"Ain't nobody playin! Line that shit up, pussy ass nigga!" said Ranada. Khafre pulled his SIG 9mm from his right pocket and began to wave it in in annoyance, causing the young women to scatter.

"You gon' get'churs, I promise you!" yelled Saudia once she was at a safe distance.

"Go get'cha brother, hoe!" yelled Khafre before watching the girls disappear around the corner. The universe must have conspired with Khafre's wishes because as soon as Khafre turned around, Saudia's brother—Kurt—stood with a .40 caliber pointed in Khafre's face, point-blank range. Khafre was in shock as the world seemed to slow down gradually. He was one hundred percent certain that his life was over until Kurt did something that Khafre would forever be grateful for. Afraid of what a hole looks like in the human head, Kurt turned his head, looking away before pulling the trigger. *Boc!* *Boc! Boc!* Kurt let off three shots, then turned back around to survey the damage. To his astonishment, Khafre wasn't there. He'd pivoted to Kurt's right, and now had his SIG to Kurt's temple.

"You played." *Boc!* Khafre put one in Kurt's head, dropping him on the side of the road like yesterday's trash. He then trotted back towards Shenida's house in a pensive state.

Once Khafre reached 31st and Avenue F, he noticed a truck that was parked on the corner. As he got closer, he realized that it was his G-ma, Shenida. She flashed her lights, signaling Khafre to get in, which he did. Shenida had watched the whole killing unfold. She knew Kurt would attempt to avenge the pain and embarrassment that Khafre had inflicted upon him. That was her whole reason for giving Khafre the SIG 9mm and asking him to walk Nilya to the bus stop.

"You okay?" asked Shenida.

"Yes, ma'am. You saw that?"

"Yeah, I saw it."

"He almost got me. Huh?"

"*Almost* don't count, baby. You did good. Now, we gotta prepare for the worst," Shenida stated while pulling off. Khafre had caught his second body in less than twenty-four hours.

Khufu

Chapter Ten

Look At What You Did

Eight days later, Khafre's suspension from school was over. He sat in the back of his homeroom class, strolling down Facebook for the latest gossip. Nilya had told Khafre that there were whispers of him killing Kurt, but nobody said anything to Khafre personally. As he continued to stroll down Facebook, he saw how many people mourned pink lip Joe and Kurt. The sight of everyone grieving over the lives that he'd took gave Khafre a different type of feeling than the actual killings. Khafre now felt intrepid and full of invigoration.

"Moss! Since you have so much time to be in your phone, come up here and find the adjective in the sentence I've put on the board," said Ms. Bucannon.

"Do you mean the word used to modify a noun, or other substantive! No problem," replied Khafre, getting up to go to the front of the class. As soon as Khafre grabbed the chalk, two detectives entered the classroom.

"Ms. Bucannon! Do you have a Moss present in here today? Khafre Moss, actually?"

"As a matter of fact, he's right here at the chalkboard."

"Mr. Moss, come with us," said Detective Archie. Khafre underlined the adjective in the sentence, then left with the detectives, leaving his fellow classmates astounded.

The drive to the police station was an irritable one for Khafre. Detective Archie attempted to make small talk, trying to be the good cop, but Khafre could see through the antics. He knew the situation was graver than they let on. Once in the interrogation room, Detective Archie fired question after question with no let-up. Khafre just listened with a blank stare on his face, until Archie took a second to drink from his water bottle.

"Listen, man, y'all pulled me outta school and I haven't even eaten anything," said Khafre.

"Oh, so you're hungry?" asked Archie.

"Yes, sir."

"Sit tight. I'll get'chu a bite to eat," stated Detective Archie, leaving the room. The other homicide detective watched Khafre on camera to see any signs of worry or uneasiness, but Khafre was as calm as a lake. About fifteen minutes later, Detective Archie walked back in the room with a bag of McDonald's and handed it to Khafre.

"Here you go, buddy."

"Thank you, detective," replied Khafre, opening the bag and going to work on the burger and fries.

"Man, you must have been really hungry."

Khafre nodded.

"So you ready to talk to me yet?"

"I need something to drink," said Khafre.

"I got'chu, buddy." Archie left and came back with a can of coke soda. Khafre wasted no time guzzling down the whole can.

"Okay. The sooner you tell me what happened the sooner you go home, lil' homie," said Archie. Khafre stretched then laid his head on the table, preparing to take a nap. This angered Archie.

"You lil' shit! You going to prison for the rest of your life! You know what they do to lil' shit like you in prison? We have the whole killing on tape, and two girls saying they saw you at the bus stop! Here, look at what'chu did to this kid, you lil' fuck!" yelled Detective Archie, pulling photos of Kurt's body out of an envelope and passing them towards Khafre. Khafre looked at the pictures then laid his head back down on the table and closed his eyes. Moments later the door opened.

"Khafre, don't say anything! Detective Archie, my client is a minor. You can't question him without parental assistance, but I'm sure you know the law. You don't have enough to hold my client anyway. Khafre, get up, let's go," stated Khafre's attorney—Willie Gary.

"It was nice meeting you, detective. Thanks for the mickey D's," stated Khafre as he left. When homicide detectives came and got Khafre from school, Nilya had seen them walking him off campus and called Shenida. She was in the parking lot of the police station waiting when Khafre came out.

***

During the ride home from the police station, Khafre was emotionless and calm as if this wasn't his first time being interrogated for murder. He'd kept his mouth closed, and Shenida disclosed to him how proud she was. Pulling in front of Shantel's home, Shenida put the truck in park, and dug in her Chanel bag.

"Here, Khafre," said Shenida, handing him a thousand dollars.

"What's this for, G-ma?" asked Khafre, puzzled and excited. He'd never held that much money at once.

"That's for you. Do what you please wit' it."

"Thank you, G-ma. You a real one."

"I know this! I told you whenever you need me I'm here. As for that lil' situation you ain't gotta worry about that. They won't be pullin' up on you no more."

"Thank you. I love you, G-ma."

"G-ma love you, too."

"I'ma call you tomorrow," Khafre stated before exiting the vehicle and heading in the house. When Khafre entered the house, Shantel was engaged in an intense conversation. From the sound of it, Shantel was on the phone with his father. When Shantel noticed Khafre, she shot him a look of disbelief, and pointed to the couch for him to have a seat.

"Look, G, I love you, but fifteen years—I can't do it. Yeah, I know, but that appeal shit ain't no guarantee. I'm not happy. Just please—let me go! Yeah, he just walked in the house. I—" *Click!* G hung the phone up on Shantel. Shantel made her way over to Khafre to explain what just took place.

"Khafre, me and yo' father—"

"Save it, mama. I'on even wanna hear it."

"Boy, who you think yo' talkin' to?" Shantel asked, drilling Khafre with her eyes.

"No disrespect, mama. I just don't wanna hear nothin' 'bout you and daddy."

"Oh yeah! What about murder? Huh? You wanna talk about that? So you went from killin' dogs to killin' people?"

"You know why I killed that dog, mama. As for that nigga, it was either him or me. He pulled a gun on me but he played. I didn't. Simple as that!"

"As simple as that? Khafre, you are thirteen years old! What the fuck is wrong wit'chu?" questioned Shantel with pure concern.

"I'm different. You know that, mama. I don't mean to be rude or nothin', but I'm exhausted. I just wanna lay down, mama," said Khafre, going in his pocket and counting out five-hundred dollars.

"Here, this for half of the rent." Khafre left the money on the couch and headed to his room. Shantel sat on her couch in mixed emotions. She was in a state of despair because of the path Khafre was taking, but was also in adulation of the young man he'd become. Shantel grabbed the money and tucked it in her bra.

Khafre entered his room, dropped his Loius Vuitton bag on the floor and stretched out over his Egyption cotton sheets. It had been a long eventful day for him. Now all Khafre wanted to do was, relax. He put his phone on *David Lyndon Huff* and tried to fall into a meditative state, but his mind kept re-painting the pictures Detective Archie pushed in front of him. The pictures of Kurt's frail body were so gory and graphic, that the hairs on Khafre's arm and neck began to rise out of pure excitement. The sound of his phone ringing broke his trance. Looking at the unknown number, Khafre didn't want to answer at first, but accepted anyway and saw that it was his father on face time.

"Pops! What up? Man, I miss you so much. I need you out here, wit' me."

"What's up wit' it? I miss you too. I'ma need you to be a lil' patient, wit' me. A'ight? It'll all be over soon," explained G.

"I hear you, pops. I see you gotta phone now. It's good to see your face. Ya dreads almost as long as mines."

"Yeah, you know I gotta keep it black, nappy and divine. King shit!" said G.

"Black, nappy and divine—I like that," said Khafre.

"As you should."

"So you and mama separated now?"

"Yeah, Khafre. I can't make her put her life on hold for some-thin' I did."

"But you did it to protect me," declared Khafre.

"And I'll do it again kuz yo' my son and I love you. Regardless of who I did it for, Khafre, I made a choice and now I gotta live wit' it. That's what real men do."

"I love you, pops. Fifteen years is a long time though."

"I won't do the whole fifteen but even if I do, always remember—no matter where you go there you are."

"What'chu mean, pop?"

"What I'm sayin' is—no matter where I go, I'ma be unapolo-getically me. I'm here now, ain't no need to cry 'bout it. You un-derstand?"

"Yes, sir, I understand."

"Enough about me. What's good wit'chu?"

"I'm just coolin', pop."

"Anything you need to tell me?"

"I'm sure G-ma Shenida told you already, pop."

"So that's what we doin' now?" asked G.

"I didn't go lookin' for that, pop. It found me," explained Khafre.

"How you feel about it?" questioned G, anxious to know the mind of his young killer.

"To be honest, pop, I feel alive everytime."

"Everytime?" G asked, surprised. There was a fleeting silence until Khafre spoke up.

"Yeah, pop, only two. You mad at me?"

"Nah. You my son. I support whatever you do in life. I just want'chu to know that once you go that route ain't no comin' back from that. Always remember it's only a sin if you feel guilty. Make sure it was well deserved, or it's gon' haunt you. You hear me?"

"I understand fully, pops. Thank you for supporting and being here for me. I love you, pops."

"I love you too. Make sure you stay in school. Do what'chu do, but make sure you go to them crakz shit, and show them who you are."

"I got'chu, pops."

"So what'chu think of Shenida?" asked G.

"Aw, man, I love her."

"Yeah, I knew you would. Listen, I'ma call you in a few days. Now that you in the field, make sure you stay outta harm's way. Don't let a nigga kill you kuz if you do, I'ma piss on yo' grave. You hear me?"

"I hear you, pop. Outta harm's way."

"All the time."

Chapter Eleven

Run Him Up

G hung up his phone and pondered on the conversation he just had with his son. Even though Khafre was only thirteen, G was receptive to what his son had become. He could identify with Khafre's demons because he too was a child killer. After realizing he'd been in the room with the window covered for a while, G got up and put his phone in the hole he'd paid maintenance to put in the wall behind his locker. As soon as G removed the towel from the window, Aaron entered the cell.

"What's up bitch? You good? Everythang good at home?" asked Aaron with genuine concern.

"Man, my son out there hittin' shit."

"Yeah? Shid! You know how shit go. You ain't there to guide him. How old you say he is?"

"My lil' man's thirteen."

"Damn! That's a lil' premature to be on that type of flex. But then again y'all from that small ass city. Y'all ain't got nothin' better to do than kill each other," stated Aaron.

"Yeah, that's some wild shit. We can't even have a mall, kuz niggas from opposite sets kept killn' each other in there. That shit illogical but it is what it is," asserted G.

"You got shit in the court, right?"

"Yeah."

"Just keep fightin'. Some shit fall through. Shid! Bitch, you'll be back out there like you never left. I came in here to tell you something. Oh yeah, bitch, the homie from yo' way—his paperwork came back today. He hot. Since he from yo' way, they want'chu to run 'em up. I wanna run 'em up wit' chu, but I gotta hold the cell down till you come back out."

"Damn! Bra a fuckin' rat? I told fool don't take my care packet if he hot. Don't trip, I got 'em," said G.

"Boom said he wanna run 'em up wit' cha."

"Nah. I'on want nobody to touch 'em. I got 'em," declared G as he got up and started packing his belongings.

***

G never understood how someone could smoke a piece of paper that was sprayed with fentanyl, heroin, horse tranquilizer, and roach spray. Even though he couldn't understand it, it didn't stop him from distributing it to the whole compound. G had given Foolie a whole strip of tunchi for free. After smoking half of the strip, Foolie sat in front of the TV in a somnolent state. Everybody in the block knew that Foolie was a marked man, except him. That's how it operates in the pen. Everybody is warned so that they can get their ice, hot water, snacks, drugs, emails and phone calls in before the yard is blown up. With cookie crumbs in the corner of his mouth, Foolie sat in front of the TV oblivious to his vulnerability. G crept up on him with superior stealth, lock and sock in hand. *Crack!* G wacked Foolie across his head with the lock, awakening him from the stupor mind set he was in. Foolie hollered and struck out immediately but tripped over his own feet. G pursued and was all over him, kicking and hitting Foolie relentlessly with the lock. Foolie screamed sounds of anguish but no one came to his rescue. Even the officer sat and watched from the officers' station as G tortured Foolie. He understood the politics of the land, and would only call for assistance when it was over.

'Ol' bitch ass nigga! Go tell the police you gotta go up top! Don't come back out. You come out, I'ma kill you!" promised G, kicking Foolie in the face. While Foolie made his way to the office, G slid under the stairs away from the camera and passed the bloody sock and lock to Aaron. He then found a seat and waited for the goon squad to come get him.

Chapter Twelve

Candle Lighting

It was a breezy Monday night. The moon was full, traffic mild, and the streets bestial as always. A crowd a little over fifty people gathered at Kurt's memorial to have a candle lighting in his remembrance. Young women wailed in agony while a few of Kurt's comrades promised Kurt's mother that she would not be the only one crying.

"Don't worry 'bout nothin', Ms. Ionis! We gon' ride for Kurt. We know the nigga who did it," declared Poo Poo, riling up the crowd.

"Kurtis was my only son! He was a good person. Even though I'm in a lot of pain, I don't want y'all out here killing up people. Just let God deal with it," announced Kurt's mother.

"Ain't nothing' wrong wit' lettin God deal with', it Ms. Ionis. We just gon' help 'em out a lil' bit," replied Poo Poo.

"This is just too much!" said Saudia, Kurt's sister. Saudia walked from the front of the crowd to the very back of it to grieve alone. With her back towards the crowd, Saudia began to have a conversation with her God.

"Lord, please give me the strength to make it through this. Why did you take my only brother, Lord? I know you said don't question yo' Lord, but why, Lord?" cried Saudia. Moments later, Saudia felt an arm around her, followed by words of comfort.

"It's gon' be okay, ma. Niggas die everyday. We can't control that." That outlandish statement caused Saudia to look up and see who was attempting to comfort her. It was an attractive young man wit a hoodie on. His face was familiar but she couldn't put a name with it. By the time she realized it was the same person who buried her face in the dirt with a gun to her head, it was too late. Khafre clutched a Glock 23 through his hoodie and had it buried in Saudia's side.

"You move wrong, they gon' be lightin' candles for yo' ass next. Understand?" Saudia nodded. "The next time you mention my name to the police, I'ma kill yo' mama and everything 'round you. You understand what I'm tellin' you?" whispered Khafre in Saudia's ear.

"Yes. I won't say anything. I promise," Saudia muttered, trembling uncontrollably.

"Good." *Boc! Boc! Boc!* Khafre let off three shots in the air, causing panic amongst the grieving. While Kurt's friends and loved ones scattered every which way, Khafre dropped to one knee and took aim at Poo Poo. Once he lined Poo Poo up in the sight of his Glock, he exhaled and squeezed off three shots, dropping Poo Poo. Khafre sprinted over to Poo Poo and stood over him.

"You gon' ride for Kurt, huh?" Khafre asked sardonically. Poo Poo rolled over on his back while clutching his chest, reminding Khafre of the scene from *Boyz in the Hood*.

"I don't even know you, man," cried Poo Poo.

"I'm the nigga that killed yo' homie." *Boc! Boc!* Khaffre hit Poo Poo twice in the head then ran through the B.G's (Bookers Garden). Once he was on the other side of the apartment complex, he jumped three gates and was in the back of Shenida's house. He'd left the back door open before attending Kurt's candle lighting. When Khafre entered the house, Shenida was sitting at her kitchen table smoking a blunt, while strolling down Facebook.

"What up, G-ma?"

"Don't *what up G-ma* me. I heard those shots. That was you?" Shenida asked above a whisper. Khafre nodded. Blowing smoke out of her nose, Shenida held her hand out.

"Give it to me." Khafre pulled the Glock 23 from his hoodie and gave it to Shenida.

"You know what to do," stated Shenida, grabbing her car keys and heading out to get rid of the murder weapon.

***

Instead of using the bathroom in the hallway, Khafre headed to Nilya's room. When Khafre entered her room, he found Nilya on her phone dressed in t-shirt and panties. The t-shirt sat right above Nilya's plumped cameltoe, and she made no effort to cover up.

"Nobody don't wanna see that. Cover that stuff up, girl!"

"Boy, you is in my room! You know you like what'chu see anyway," taunted Nilya, patting her pussy.

"I really don't. Let me use yo' shower."

"Don't leave my tub dirty, big head. Go ahead." Khafre entered the bathroom, removed his clothing, took a minute to gaze at the man in the mirror that he was becoming, then finally got in the shower. The hot water stimulated every muscle in Khafre's back as he closed his eyes and replayed the events of the day. Khafre was in such deep thought, that he didn't hear Nilya enter the bathroom fully naked. When Nilya stepped into the shower, Khafre's eyes were still closed. She glanced down at Khafre's manhood and was frightened and excited all at once. Nilya placing a firm grip around Khafre's dick, causing Khafre to tense up and open his eyes.

"Girl, what'chu—" Nilya put her right hand over Khafre's mouth.

"Shhh, relax. I got'chu," said Nilya, then she removed her hand from his mouth and kissed him passionately while jacking his dick slowly. Khafre moaned in ecstasy and grabbed both of Nilya's plump cheeks, pulling her close. Nilya placed her left leg on the edge of the tub and began to rub the head of Khafre's dick on her clit.

"Umm—Khafre, let me taste it please." Nilya dropped to her knees and began to suck Khafre's dick and massage it at the same time. Khafre shivered and damn near buckled while making sounds that were effeminate. Before Khafre could cum, Nilya snatched his dick out of her mouth and stood up.

"Come on," said Nilya, pulling Khafre by the arm, leading him to her bed, never turning the shower off. Nilya crawled in her bed like a feline, seductively put an arch in her back and swayed her hips from side to side, enticing Khafre. Nilya's body and skin tone was flawless. The way her pussy lips rested up under her pubes like fresh ripened fruit stirred something in Khafre. He crawled in bed behind her, still dripping wet from the shower, and buried his face in Nilya's love nest.

"Ahhh—sss—ooo—Khafre, yes!" *This can't be his first time*, thought Nilya as Khafre made her clitoris dance. Khafre's dick pulsated with anticipation while Nilya moaned every vowel known to man. He continued to demonstrate what he'd seen on Porn Hub so many times, forcing Nilya to communicate with God.

"Sss—ooo—my God—Khafre baby, I'm nuttin'!" groaned Nilya while having spasms like an epileptic. Khafre sucked up everything Nilya's body produced, until she collapsed on her stomach in unimaginable gratification. Before she could gather herself, Khafre slid in her from behind nice and easy. He eased the head of his dick in and out of Nilya, going a little deeper, each stroke sending a chill up Nilya's spine.

"Whoooooo—sss—Hiiii—shit! Khafre, you in this pussy!" moaned Nilya while gripping her Versace pillow.

"Damn, Nilya!" groaned Khafre. Nilya's pussy was so wet and warm. It gripped every inch of Khafre's dick, causing him to make grotesque faces.

On the verge of cumming, Khafre snatched out of Nilya, and slapped her ass cheeks with his dick in an attempt to calm himself and avoid cumming prematurely. He then grabbed Nilya's left leg and flipped her on her back.

"Umm—give it to me, please!" cried Nilya. Khafre entered her again, caressing her velvet-soft body with every stroke.

"Sshh—sss—ooo—baby, yes!" Nilya and Khafre's moans resembled a love song. Even though this was the first time for both of them, their bodies moved in unison to a delectable rhythm. Caught up in the moment, neither of them realized that Nilya was bleeding. For the next thirty minutes they pushed, pulled, and groaned until they were both demolished by orgasms. Unbeknownst to them both, Shenida was on the other side of the door overhearing everything. In a weird way, listening to Khafre put it down turned her on. Shenida made her way to her room and found herself playing in her pussy while thinking of Khafre.

Chapter Thirteen

Welcome To Florida

Three Years Later—

Khafre pulled into Centennial High School in a new Benz truck that Shenida had bought him for his sixteenth birthday. He was now in the ninth grade, with a reputation that preceded itself. Everybody knew that Khafre had killed Kurt and got away with it. He was loved and adored by beautiful women, young and old, but hated and feared by men of his peers. Within the first nine weeks of school, Khafre had a crew consolidated. He took a liking to two cousins who had moved from Liberty City to Miami, Lil' Reese and Quay. Lil' Reese bore a striking resemblance to Jody Breeze from the rap group "Boyz-N-Da Hood", with a laid-back demeanor. His M.O. was: sticking up franchises. However, Quay was way different. He was tall, light-skinned, with shoulder-length dreadlocks. What with his large face and a big nose, Khafre often teased Quay, calling him *face man*. Quay's M.O. was: robbing dope boys and armor trucks. He was only sixteen and had already been shot nine times.

Even though Quay was a live wire, Khafre still embraced him. He felt as if every crew needed that one wild nigga to set shit off. When Khafre walked on campus, Lil' Reese and Quay were posted at the entrance, waiting on him.

"What's up, my guy?" greeted Lil' Reese, dappin' Khafre up.

"What's good wit' you boys?" asked Khafre.

"Shid—you tell me! You da one pullin' up hoppin' outta G-Wagons and shit. What up? Put a nigga on, let me hold somethin'," said Quay, drawing attention with his theatrics.

"I stay wit' that work, if you need a job, nigga," Khafre stated, smiling arrogantly.

"Oh, don't get flippant wit' me, nigga! I stay banked up," replied Quay, pulling out a nice wad of money.

"Nigga, that's a Haitian knot! You got one, one-hunid dollar bill on the top wit' two-hunid one's in the middle," proclaimed Khafre.

"You gotta real nigga fucked up," Quay declared, putting the money back in his pocket.

"If them was all hunnids, nigga, you woulda spread it! Like I said, nigga that's about three-hunnid dollars," Khafre stated, walking off with Lil' Reese and Quay behind him.

"Y'all boys cloyin' early dis mornin' and shit. All deez beautiful tenders scattered around out here, and you niggaz arguin' bout nothin'! Look at all dis stuff out here!" said Lil' Reese, referring to the women. "Speaking of tenders, there go yours over there." Reese nodded towards Nilya.

"That ain't my girl. That's just my ride or die," said Khafre.

"Man! Stop what'chu doin', fool. Everybody know you and Nilya fuckin', fool," replied Reese. Khafre laughed wickedly at Reese's comment before approaching Nilya.

"Hey, big head," Nilya said, smiling fervently.

"What's up wit' it? Let me scream at'cha for a minute." Without saying anything to her boyfriend, Dirk, Nilya walked off with Khafre. Dirk exhaled dramatically, throwing his hands in the air hopelessly.

"What? Wassup? You straight? Nigga, you even act like you gotta problem wit' my homie hollin' at'cha bitch. Nigga, I'll do it ta ya ass out here, boy!" Quay pointed his finger in Dirk's face. Lil' Reese stood on the side of Quay, bouncing like a gangsta and taunting Dirk, hoping he took the bait. Dirk maintained his composure. He wasn't stupid. Everybody knew that Khafre was a killer, and if you rolled with him, you had to be one too.

"What's up, Khafre? What'chu, gotta holla at me 'bout?" asked Nilya.

"Nothin'. You look like you needed saving, so I put ma lil' cape on and swung through."

"Boy, please! You is too much!" said Nilya, smiling.

"Man, yo' whole vibe, body language and all was screamin' *save me*! Why you fuck wit' dude anyway? He ain't even yo' type."

"Jealousy don't look good on you, boo boo," said Nilya, squeezing Khafre's right cheek. Khafre brushed her hand away.

"You sound real crazy right now. I can get that muscle between yo' thighs when I feel like it," boasted Khafre.

"You can most definitely get dis pussy whenever, but Dirk— he got my mind."

"Then why you over here wit' me?"

"You tell me," replied Nilya, grinning.

"Man, I just wanted to know if you ridin' home wit' me."

"In what?"

"Yesterday I grabbed a G-wagon."

"I'm not ridin' in no stolen car you and yo' lil' crew done picked up."

"My shit fresh off the lot—paperwork on deck. Fuck you mean?"

"I'on know. I was suppose' to ride home wit' Dirk. I'll let'chu know before school out," said Nilya, attempting to walk off. Khafre grabbed Nilya by the hand and pulled her close. He then wrapped his hands around her neck in a firm grip and kissed her deepily.

"That's what da fuck um talkin' 'bout! Do that shit, homeboy!" yelled Reese.

"Hmm—you a trip. I gotta whole boyfriend over there. You gone just thug me like that?"

"I'll see you in the parkin' lot," asserted Khafre.

"Period," replied Nilya, walking away and heading towards Dirk.

"Y'all niggaz, come on!" ordered Khafre.

***

Instead of going to class, Khafre and Lil' Reese were in the bathroom twisting up gravel leafs and taking shots of Remy, while Quay shot craps with two New York niggas.

"Aye, check me out. I got two bricks of molly I'ma drop on you and Quay. Y'all just bring me seventy-five a piece— we good," stated Khafre.

"Look, since you presented the proposition, outta respect for you, we gon' take it this time. We don't really fuck wit' dis dope shit, kuz too much come wit' it. We let other niggaz move dis shit, then go take all da money. You know our M.O.," declared Reese.

"I'on fuck wit' dope neither. This shit just fell in my lap. I had to see if you boyz was good. It's only right."

"Give us a week or two—we'll move it," assured Reese, putting flame to his blunt.

"Yo, son! Yo' dice game mad goofy yo!" clowned Grit, drawing laughter from his homie—Seth.

"Yoooo—you niggaz is mad wild! Y'all got the bliky'z in school? Shit ain't that serious yo!" pronounced Grit.

"Shut da fuck up, fa I heat'cha azz up in dis bitch!" ordered Quay, taking Grit's money and jewels. With no words, Reese followed suit—taking Seth's possessions as well. Khafre just stood back smoking a blunt, waving his Glock back and forth from Grit to Seth.

"Welcome to Florida! Gun shine state, baby!" boasted Quay.

"Y'all niggaz stay put. Keep ya ass in here until the bell rang. Anyone of you niggaz move, I'ma go to movin' organs and nerves around," declared Reese, as the trio departed from the restroom.

Khafre was the only black student in his honor's class that learned history. His teacher—Mr. Stanton—despised him for being a flamboyant, intellectual young black man. On top of that, Khafre was late to his class everyday. As soon as Khafre entered the classroom, dripping in gold and designer apparel, Mr. Stanton stopped his sermon on the Pilgrims and Indians, and instantly became flushed and beet-red.

"Get out!" yelled Mr. Stanton, startling a few of his students.

"I seen that movie for the first-time last night," Khafre proclaimed. "It really depicts the betrayal and savage mind set of the Europeans. Speakin' of betrayal—don't forget to enlighten yo' students on how the Pilgrims betrayed the peaceful Indians. Tell 'em how the Pilgrims gifted the Indians with blankets that were contaminated with smallpox. Tell 'em how the Indians were here in America before Columbus, and how the Pilgrims got the Indians drunk, slaughtered them for the land and called it *Thanksgiving*. And—most importantly—make sure you tell yo' precious white students that their so-called superior skin is really a skin deficiency. Let 'em know that Europeans are an endangered species—you souless self-hatin' pussy." Khafre pressed the black button that alerted the front office and left the classroom.

Khufu

Chapter Fourteen

In School Suspension

"Khafre Le Grand Moss! In my office now!" Khafre got up and headed in the dean's office. "Close the door and have a seat!" Khafre did as he was told. "What is your problem?" asked Ms. Cramtree while pulling Khafre's dick out of his Hugo sweats.

"I's been a bad nigger, maaser," asserted Khafre role- playing.

"Don't I know it," replied Ms. Cramtree, dropping to her knees and swallowing Khafre's shaft whole. Ms. Cramtree was Khafre's fifth grade teacher. She was now a dean at Centennial High School. Intrigued by Khafre's intellect, Ms. Cramtree had been having sexual relations with Khafre for six months. Raised on racist ethics, Ms. Cramtree was curious as to why her father was so adamant about not fucking with blacks. After getting a dose of Khafre, she now knew why.

"Sss—shin—shit. Thats it, eat it up," demanded Khafre, holding Ms. Cramtree by her hair as he fucked her face mercilessly. Ms. Cramtree gagged periodically, but that didn't wane her performance. Knowing that their time was limited, Khafre snatched her mouth off of his dick and put a condom on. He then stood up, bent her over, pinned her head to the desk and entered her cruelly. Ms. Cramtree bit her bottom lip and gripped her office desk, trying her hardest to muffle her sounds.

"Hmmm—Uhh—hmm," moaned Ms. Cramtree. Normally, Khafre was soundless and quick to cum before someone noticed that he was craming Ms. Cramtree, but today her pussy was wetter than usual, causing Khafre to be reckless.

"What'chu love?"

"Black cock!"

"What matters?"

"Black lives!" moaned Ms. Cramtree as she and Khafre orgasmed simultaneously. With no words Khafre pulled out of her, pulled his pants up and headed out the door.

"Go have a seat in ISS until school is over!" yelled Ms. Cramtree, attempting to fix her hair.

"Is everything okay, Ms. Cramtree?" asked Ms. Snider, the school's secretary.

"Everything's fine!" retorted Ms. Cramtree, slamming the door to her office.

***

"I ain't gon' even front, this G-wagon looks good on you," Nilya admitted, gazing at Khafre in a flirtatious manner.

"I know dis!" replied Khafre arrogantly, showing all thirty-two of his pearly whites.

"Damn, Khafre. You gotta beautiful smile. You should smile more often," said Nilya, reaching for Khafre's zipper.

"What'chu doin'?" asked Khafre, pushing Nilya's hand away.

"What it look like? You can't drive and get'cha dick sucked at the same time?"

"It ain't that. Trust me, I would love for you to wrap them pretty ass lips around this log."

"Then what is it?" Khafre glanced out of his window, then focused his attention back on the road, gripping the steering wheel tightly before answering Nilya.

"Ms. Cramtree sucked my dick earlier in her office. That's the reason I won't let'chu."

"Why is you lying on that lady?"

"I ever lied to you? Ever?" Nilya saw the seriousness in Khafre's demeanor.

"Uggg! You let that old white lady put her mouth on you?"

"The older the mouth the better the performance!"

"I seriously can't believe you right now," stated Nilya in disgust.

"Ain't nothin'. I did it for the ancestors," muttered Khafre with a smirk on his face.

"I'm pretty sure the ancestors pissed 'bout that one."

"Enough about me. What's good wit'chu and that lame ass nigga Dirk?"

"What about him?"

"Why are you with him?"

"Dirk is nice. I told you Dirk got my mind."

"What about ya heart?"

"You know you gon' always have my heart, Khafre. Us women need different men for different reasons. No one man could ever give a woman everything she needs," philosophized Nilya.

"Is that right?" questioned Khafre, as he turned right on 23rd and noticed something that disturbed him deeply.

"What'chu slowin' down for?" asked Nilya.

"You see that?"

"Yeah, I see it but what we gon' do about it? He the damn police!" exclaimed Nilya.

"I'm so fuckin tired of these crackers playin' duck hunt wit' us! All that marching and shit played out!" stated Khafre, making a right on 22nd Avenue. Khafre had been watching YouTube videos of all blacks slain by racist cops. The one that took him over the edge was the murder of George Floyd. Khafre pulled the truck over to the curb and put it in *park*.

"What'chu doin'?" asked Nilya. Khafre ignored her and reached in the back seat for his hoodie and SIG .40 caliber.

"Get in the driver seat. I'll be right back," said Khafre, hopping out the truck before Nilya could contest his order. Khafre cut through an old friend's yard and stepped over a fence that had been down for years. Once he rounded the project house, he saw that the same police officer had a little girl's face buried in the concrete. He attempted to put handcuffs on her but she resisted peevishly while crying for help. Her wailing made Khafre's skin crawl and filled him with rage.

"Stop resisting!" yelled the rookie cop who hadn't called for back up yet.

"I didn't do nothing! You hurting me!" cried Drea.

"Hey!" yelled Khafre. The officer looked up and found himself staring at his future. *Boc!* Khafre hit the officer in the head, causing him to slump over the little girl. Khafre grabbed the officer's shirt and pulled his limp body off of Drea.

"Get up," ordered Khafre, pulling Drea up by the hand. Drea glanced at Khafre then took off. *Boc! Boc! Boc!* Khafre put three more holes in what was left of the cop's head then took off. When Khafre hopped back in his truck, Nilya put it in gear and pulled off. She was well aware that she was now an accessory to murder.

Chapter Fifteen

I Want In

After getting rid of the murder weapon, Khafre went home with Nilya. He laid comfortably in her bed, smoking a blunt while gazing at the ceiling. With various thoughts circling his mind, Khafre didn't notice Nilya staring at him with mixed feelings. She was in awe, terrified, and confused all at once. Knowing that Khafre had put his life on the line to save a young woman had Nilya's juices flowing. She removed the blunt from his mouth, placed it in hers and stradled him. After taking a few tokes, Nilya leaned over and put the blunt out in the astray that was on her bedside dresser.

"Khafre, I want a part of what you got goin' on."

"What'chu mean? And why the hell you put the blunt out?"

"I gotta feelin' that you finna embark on some wild shit, and I want in," Nilya stated as she rubbed Khafre's chest and grinded on him provocatively.

"What'chu need to focus on is graduating next year and headin' to college."

"College can wait. I heard and felt what you said in the car today. I agree wit'chu wholeheartedly. Marching is obsolete. Bloodshed is the only language they understand."

"I said no!" replied Khafre. Nilya leaned forward, grabbed Khafre's dick and navigated it to her juicy fruit. She wiggled down on every inch, drawing moans of pleasure from Khafre. For the next thirty minutes, Nilya gave Khafre everything she had as if their sex organs were at war. By the end of multiple orgasms, Khafre had given in to Nilya's wishes. She would be joining him on a murderous escapade.

***

Nilya laid anxiously on the sofa in a house that her and Khafre had been casing for a week. The house belonged to a middle-class old Italian woman who vacationed frequently. Khafre knew that the homeowner was out of town because the trash hadn't been pulled along aside the road, and the mailbox was overflowing with mail. A knock at the door caused Nilya to tense up. Remembering the cause she was sacrificing for, Nilya inhaled through her nose and exhaled out of her mouth slowly to calm her nerves.

"Just a minute!" yelled Nilya as she fancied up the most seductive look that she could muster. As soon as Nilya opened the door, the black cop—who was a twenty-year veteran on the force—made a mental catalogue of Nilya's sensuous beauty. After a slight suspension of time and reality, the black cop's white partner cleared his throat, bringing his partner back to existence.

"Ah—yeah. Hi, ma'am, we gotta call about a domestic. Are you okay?"

"Yeah, I'm the one who called you guys. Me and my boyfriend had an argument, but everything's okay now, he left," Nilya stated, opening and closing her robe casually, giving both officers a glimpse of her perky breasts and waxed pussy. The veteran cop shifted positions in an attempt to hide his erection.

"So, ahh—are you sure that you're okay?" Can I help you with anything else?"

"Umm—actually you can. Before you guys came I couldn't get my toilet to flush. Can you just take a look at it for me?" Nilya asked while fooling around in a dainty feminine gesture with a loose strand of hair that hung on the side of her face. The veteran cop looked back at his rookie partner with pleading eyes.

"I'll meet'chu in the car in a few minutes."

"Sure thing, partner," replied the rookie cop, winking at his partner before heading out to the police cruiser.

"Come on in, officer. The bathroom's right there to your left," Nilya directed, closing and locking the door behind her. The officer walked into the bathroom and flushed the toilet with no problem.

"Ma'am! Ma'am—the toilet works just fi—" Nilya sitting completely naked with her legs wide open caused the officer's words to be cut short.

"You mind helping me with this?" Nilya played with her clit while biting her bottom lip and rotating her hips slowly.

"Good God Almighty!" muttered the officer as his heart rate accelerated way past normal. He made his way over to the sofa, got on his knees and buried his face in Nilya's young pussy.

"Sss—ooohh—officer, you so nasty!" moaned Nilya, throwing her pussy in the cop's face. Khafre slipped out of the hallway closet and crept on stealth mode until he was close enough to do what he intended.

"George Floyd!" Khafre yelled before putting a trash bag over the cop's face. The old veteran whimpered and cried out while kicking and clawing at the trash bag but to no avail. Khafre applied pressure until there was no sign of life left. Nilya dressed quickly and wiped everything she touched. As soon as Nilya and Khafre stepped outside, Quay and Reese were opening fire on the rookie cop that sat helplessly in the police cruiser. Nilya held her hand over her mouth astoundingly as the 5.56 NATO rounds tunneled through the flesh of the cop, causing his body to recoil chaotically while still strapped in his seat belt.

"Let's move," advised Khafre, pulling Nilya by the hand and leading her towards the getaway car. After discharging their whole clips, Reese and Quay followed suit, galloping to the car with semi-automatics dangling by the waist side. Neighbors peeked out of their windows as Quay and Reese hopped in the vehicle. They tried rigorously to read the plates on the car as Khafre pulled off but to no avail. The car didn't bear any tag. Khafre and his crew slipped off into the muggy night under the Florida moon.

Khufu

Chapter Sixteen

Fish Grease

"Damn, nigga, I miss you so fuckin' much," moaned Shenida, wrapping her arms around G-Baby's neck.

"I miss you too," G-Baby replied, slipping his hand under Shenida's dress and rubbing her clit.

"Umm—she misses you, daddy. I told you I wasn't gon' wear no panties."

"Moss! Cut it out. Go ahead and have a seat," advised Ms. Washington. Ms. Washington had a thing for G-Baby. She smuggled cigarettes in for him, free of charge. G-Baby winked at Ms. Washington then put his finger in his mouth and sucked Shenida's juices from them. Ms. Washington just shook her head.

"That's ya lil' girlfriend, huh?" asked Shenida as she took a seat across from G-Baby.

"I'on know her," lied G-Baby.

"Whatever!" replied Shenida with a wave of her hand.

"So how my son movin' out there? He a'ight?" asked G-Baby, opening a bag of chips.

"Yeah, he movin' how he suppose' to. I got 'em. He got yo' blood in him so you know he thoroughbred—a natural born killa."

"Already! I gotta call 'em. I ain't spoke to him since I been out the hole."

"Wat'chu was in the hole for?"

"A nigga came here from the city. He was hot so I had to get 'em from round here."

"Wat'chu mean *hot*?" questioned Shenida, confused.

"He was a rat," explained G-Baby.

"Oh—okay. That shit ruff in there, huh?"

"Yeah, it's always tension in the air. Gotta keep a knife on me. In the shower, um sleepin' in my boots and shit. Ain't nobody goin' home. Everybody got double digits—life sentences and shit." G-Baby shook his head.

"Damn, daddy."

"It's all good, ma. You know I'ma handle me. On another note, though, tell C-major I said to spray that shit wit' another coat. I want straight gas! I'on want that shit that give 'em a weed high. I'm tryin' to make a bitch twack out!"

"Da last K-2 I sent you—he said it was gas."

"Just tell 'em what I said."

"A'ight, I got'chu."

"You still moving that molly?"

"You already know. Da city eatin' that shit up! I'on even know why you in here sellin' K-2. You left plenty of money out there that you ain't even gotta touch. I can take care of you until you come home, G-Baby!" said Shenida.

"I know. I just like to stay busy. I'm allergic to stagnation."

"Boy, read a book or somethin'."

"Shid—all I do is read and workout."

"Umm—you is lookin' all weefy and shit! I sho'll wish you could work out on dis," Shenida stated as she leaned back and opened her legs, exposing her well-waxed pussy.

"Damn. You lookin' real colossal down there. Fat pussy!" expressed Baby-G, grabbing his manhood as it grew in size.

"Come kiss it, daddy. Fuck deez crackaz." Shenida rolled her hips in slow motion, drawing attention from a few inmates who'd been watching her since they laid eyes upon her. The sound of Ms. Washington clearing her throat brought G-Baby back from lustville.

"Moss, your visitor is doing entirely too much. Say your good-byes and wrap it up—let's go," Ms. Washington whispered to G-Baby before walking off.

"I knew you was fuckin' that hoe. Why she ain't get on the radio and call it in?" asked Shenida seethingly.

"She just real cool like that, I guess. I'on know. Get up and give me a hug." Shenida got up and kissed G-Baby, making sure to stick her tongue down his throat. G-Baby obliged and grabbed a handful of Shenida's delicate perfect sized ass.

"I love you, G-Baby," moaned Shenida.

"I love you too, girl."

"Moss! Let's go!" ordered Ms. Washington.

***

When G-Baby returned from visitation, the dorm was surprisingly boisterous. G-Baby noticed his cellmate, Aaron, playing chess with P-Moe, and decided to approach him to see what the excitement was all about.

"What's good, A?" asked G-Baby.

"Just coolin', gettin' on dis nigga ass on dis chess board. You a'ight? How ya visit was?"

"I'ma tell you 'bout that shit later. I'm sayin', like—why deez niggaz so hyped up in dis bitch?" asked G-Baby, looking around curiously.

"Everybody drunk as hell off that white lightin'. I got some up there in my locker. It's in that water bottle. Go get'cha a taste."

"A'ight, be back in a minute. I got next on da chess board," G-Baby stated before heading to his cell. Once in the room, he went straight to Aaron's locker and drank a quarter of the loo proof liquor.

"Damn!" expressed G-Baby, screwing his face up at the potency of the homemade hooch. After putting the bottle back in Aaron's locker, G-Baby relieved himself of all the fluids he'd drank before visitation and heard De-Zoe arguing in the vent.

"Get'cha shit and get the fuck out my room, bitch ass nigga! Go tell dem crackers you can't be in here!" yelled De-Zoe. De-Zoe was born in Haiti and proud of his Haitian roots. He moved to Miami when he was twelve and got indicted by the Feds by the time he was twenty-four. He was sentenced to thirty years for drug related crimes. Someone close to him ratted him out, so De-Zoe had no understanding for snitches. G-Baby had met De-Zoe at the chapel when he was invited by a friend to attend an IFA class which was a religion indigenous to Africa. After washing his hands, G-Baby went to investigate. When he got to De-Zoe's room, he saw De-Zoe throwing his cellie's mat outside.

"De-Zoe, what's good?" asked G-Baby.

"Dis weak ass nigga gotta go, bra. He can't be in dis cell no more," said De-Zoe.

"You always teachin' about "black power" but'chu kickin' another black man out'cha cell. Help me understand that, De-Zoe."

"Nigga, on my indictment, it says, *The United States vs De-Zoe*!"

"I don't follow," replied G-Baby, perplexed.

"Dis nigga workin' wit' da United States! He workin' wit' dem crackaz!" proclaimed De-Zoe in his strong Haitian accent.

"Oh yeah?"

"Yeah!"

"Why you tryin' to put'em out'cha room? Just crush'em! Get'em off da pound," advised G-Baby, pulling a knife from his Khaki pants and handing it to De-Zoe.

"Dis nigga don't know who he fuckin' wit'. I'ma do dis shit for the ancestors," declared De-Zoe as he walked off casually with G-Baby behind him. De-Zoe tip-toed until he had perfect position behind his victim, and all in one motion De-Zoe slipped his arm around his cellie's neck and stabbed him in the top of his head repeatedly.

"Bitch-made-hot-fish-grease-pussy-ass nigga!" muttered De-Zoe with every stab and spurt of blood that shot from his victim's head. Everything happened so fast that his victim couldn't even process what was taking place. When De-Zoe turned him loose, he fell to the floor barely clinging on to his life. G-Baby looked around for the C.O. then kicked the dying man in the face.

"Hot ass nigga! Finish that nigga ass off," stated G-Baby before disappearing. De-Zoe dropped to his knees and planted the knife in and out of his cellie until the unit officer returned from using the restroom. Once the officer spotted De-Zoe stabbing another inmate, he hit the panic button which notified the goon squad.

"Everybody to your rooms—Now!"

Chapter Seventeen

Play God

Khafre's truck was fogged out with weed smoke as he weaved through traffic like needle and thread. Quay and Reese circulated blunts around while Nilya trolled on Facebook. They'd just gotten out of school, and were now headed to Khafre's mother's house. It had been a while since he'd checked on her. Khafre turned the music down before speaking.

"Aye, Reese!" Reese hit the blunt, then passed it to Khafre before speaking.

"Yeah, what's good?"

"Y'all moved that molly yet?" Khafre asked before taking a toke from the blunt.

"We just got rid of the last of it in school," confirmed Reese.

"Don't ask us to move no more of that shit! That shit is a fuckin' headache! All dem molly heads rustin' a nigga soon as we hit school campus. They gon' get a nigga knocked off!" whined Quay.

"You don't love money? You can't control yo' customers?" asked Khafre.

"Man—It's quicker ways to get that paper."

"I agree," said Reese.

"A'ight. I'ma see what it is. In da mean time pass that fetti up here." Reese handed Khafre the money. "Here, count dis," Khafre told Nilya, handing her the money and then passing the blunt back to Reese. When Khafre passed the blunt to Reese, he noticed Quay giving him a sullen look with a smirk on his face in the rearview mirror. Khafre made a mental note to check him later on.

"This is fifteen thousand, Khafre," said Nilya.

"Count out five and hand it to me," requested Khafre, pulling into his mother's house. After meddling with his phone, Khafre stuck it in the side of his door.

"Here, you said five thousand, right?" asked Nilya.

"Yeah, come in with me right quick." Nilya and Khafre got out and headed in the house.

***

"Bitch! You think I'm stupid or some shit?" asked Will.

"What is you talkin' about?" retorted Shantel.

"Why every time that nigga call, you gotta walk out the room? Yo' still love that nigga? Huh?" questioned Will, aggressively walking towards Shantel.

"Man—please! G-Baby got fifteen years. Why is you worried about him? You so insecure. That's my child's father. I'ma always love him. If you can't deal with that reality, then I'on know what to tell you."

"Hoe, you got me fucked up!" *Fop!* Will slapped Shantel down to the floor, causing her to shriek while holding her face. "You gon' learn to respect me! You hear me?" The sound of the bedroom door being kicked off the hinges startled Will. Khafre entered Shantel's bedroom with blood in his eyes and murder on his mind. He drew his SIG 9mm, walked past Shantel and shot Will in the knee cap. *Boc!*

"Khafre, no!" Shantel and Nilya screamed in unison. Khafre ignored them both and advanced. He stood over Will and grabbed him by his mini afro.

"Nigga, if you fuckin' wit' my mama, I know you know who my father is! And if you know who my father is you most definitely know who da fuck I am! So that tells me two thangz about'chu. Either you stupid as fuck or you a cold-blooded killer. The way you tremblin' and shit, I'ma assume you just stupid!" Khafre stated through clenched teeth then pounced on Will. Khafre hit Will with such force that one could hear the bones breaking beneath his facial flesh. Nilya had took off to get help, leaving Shantel pleading for Khafre to stop. Moments later, Quay and Reese entered the room anxiously. Nilya expected them to stop Khafre but they just joined in on the on-slaught, kicking Will in his face and ribs. Shantel screaming to the top of her lungs snapped Khafre out of his outlandish trance.

"Y'all niggaz chill! I got it. I'ma meet'chu in the truck," said Khafre. Quay stomped on Will's head once more before leaving.

"Why you bringing people in my house to jump on my friend?" asked Shantel.

"Who the fuck is dis nigga, mama?" Khafre asked with disdain in his eyes.

"Will is my friend! You ain't been by here in God knows when, but'chu wanna come in here and play God. Boy, get out my house!" With a look of disbelief, Khafre walked back over to Will, put his gun between his eyes and stared Shantel in her eyes. Shantel put her hands over her mouth and shook her head as tears flowed from her eyes.

"Khafre, don't!" cried Shantel.

"You choose dis weak ass nigga over my father?" Khafre asked with watery eyes.

"He just my friend!" Khafre turned his attention back to the barely conscious man.

"You touch my mama again, nigga, I'ma kill you! *Boc!* Khafre shot Will in his other kneecap and headed for the door. Before leaving, Khafre went in his pocket and threw the five thousand dollars on the floor next to Shantel. As he left his mother's house, he felt betrayed and a shameful immense amount of pity for her. He wondered what made his mother succumb to someone beneath his father.

Khufu

Chapter Eighteen

Snake You

Nilya caressed Khafre's right hand as he steered with his left, driving in silence. He was on his way to drop Quay and Reese off to Sable Chase. Sable Chase was a nice apartment complex that housed a lot of ratchet and grimy people that moved from the projects. Unexpectedly, Quay laughed crudely.

"That shit was lit! Yaah! We got straight on that old nigga ass! I live for this type of shit!" Quay exclaimed excitedly. Khafre glanced at Quay through the rearview mirror with murder on his mind and malice in his heart.

"Man, cool it, fool. You see Khafre ain't in the mood," muttered Reese.

"That old nigga got what he deserved. Fuck that! I know you ain't in ya feelings up there, is you?" taunted Quay. Khafre reached for his pistol on the sly, but Nilya put her hand over his and shook her head by way of saying, *No.* Khafre relaxed and continued to drive.

"You got some more of that molly?" asked Reese.

"I thought you niggaz just said y'all through wit' that. It's a headache, remember?" said Khafre.

"Change of heart, one more flip won't hurt," proclaimed Reese. Khafre saw through their facade but he obliged anyway.

"How many we talkin'?" asked Khafre.

"Shid—shoot us 'bout six of dem thangz!" Quay said. Khafre smirked with petulance.

"Say no more. I got'cha," assured Khafre, pulling in front of their apartment building.

"A'ight my guy. Hit us when you ready," said Reese before exiting Khafre's truck.

"Aye, Khafre, I hope I ain't get'chu all in ya feelings and shit. If I did, that's my bad," Quay stated plaintively.

"Ain't no pressure," replied Khafre wryly.

"Bye, Nilya," Quay uttered before getting out of the truck, but Nilya remained silent. Once Quay was out of the vehicle, Khafre put the truck in drive and handed Nilya his phone.

"What'chu want me to do wit' this?" asked Nilya.

"When we went in my mama's house, I put my phone on record. Play it back."

"Khafre, if you don't trust 'em why you got 'em around you?" questioned Nilya.

"Dis shit chess, Nilya. You gotta be strategic wit' dis shit. Now, play the recorder back." Nilya reclined her seat, put her legs on the dashboard and played the recorder.

Quay: *Whatz up wit' dis clown ass nigga man?*
Reese: *What'chu mean, fool?*
Quay: *Dis nigga, Khafre, think he the Godfather of some shit. I'm gettin' tired of being round dis lame ass nigga anyway. What type of name is Khafre? Shit lame as hell!*
Reese: *You trippin', fool. Bra a good nigga.*
Quay: *Man, fuck all that! Get dis nigga to front us some more bricks of molly and we just gone take that shit.*
Reese: *If we do that, we gon' have to kill 'em. Fool a dangerous nigga.*
Quay: *Nigga, I'ma killa too.*
Reese: *I fuck wit' fool but you my people. If dis what'chuwana do, I'm ridin' wit'cha. Fuckit!*
Quay: *Hold up. There go, Nilya!*

"Stop that shit. Cut it off. I heard enough," Khafre said as fury spread throughout his entire being.

"I'm sorry, Khafre," exclaimed Nilya, rubbing Khafre's back.

"I'm not the one you should be feeling sorry for."

"What'chu gon' do, Khafre?" asked Nilya with bated breath.

"I'm a charitable man, shid! I'ma give 'em what they want." Khafre's phone rang.

"It's my mama," said Nilya.

"Answer it, put it on speaker phone."

"Hey, ma!"

"What' up, Nilya? What'chu doing wit' Khafre's phone?" questioned Shenida.

"Oh, he was doin' somethin', so I just answered the phone for him."

"Where he at?"

"What's good, G-ma?" asked Khafre.

"Hey, baby. What y'all doin?"

"We just bendin' through da city baskin' in da ambience," replied Khafre.

"Baskin' in da *ambience*, huh?" asked Shenida with a mild chuckle. "Listen, I need you to take care of somethin' for me. Drop Nilya off, and I'ma drop you *addy* to where I'm at."

"A'igh't, G-ma," replied Khafre.

"I'll see you when I get home, Nilya."

"Okay, mama, love you."

"Love you too," stated Shenida. Nilya hung up the phone and gazed at Khafre.

"What'chu and my mama be doin'?" questioned Nilya, lips tightening with curiosity.

"Bidness," answered Khafre in a molly tone.

"What kind of bidness?"

"A lil' dis a lil' that," Khafre stated nonchalantly.

"You ever killed somebody wit' my mama before?" Khafre said nothing but gave Nilya a look of recognition before pulling into her driveway. Nilya kissed the back of her teeth seethingly with envy.

"I wanna experience that wit'chu, so when you gon' let me kill wit'chu?" said Nilya.

"You already experience that wit' me, remember?" asked Khafre.

"Yeah, but I didn't get to take life—you did, remember?" replied Nilya sardonically.

"Listen, we'll discuss dis later."

"Whatever!"

"Come here," demanded Khafre. Nilya leaned in, pouting.

"What?" asked Nilya. Khafre grabbed Nilya under her chin and kissed her passionately. Nilya moaned in pleasure before Khafre unlocked his lips from hers.

"Come in real quick! Please," moaned Nilya.

"I gotta go. I'ma pull up on you later. I love you."

"You make me sick. I love you too," said Nilya before getting out of Khafre's truck.

***

When Khafre pulled into the Brown Store, his phone started to ring.

"Hello!"

"I see you just pulled in. Pull 'round da back of the store, and come up the stairs," instructed Shenida.

"A'ight," replied Khafre, pulling around the back. He wondered why Shenida wanted him to meet her in the back of the store. He had no idea that the apartment on top of the Brown Store was his father's home away from home. Khafre killed the engine and hopped out with a .40 on his waist. When he rounded the back of the store, Shenida was waiting at the top of the steps in a satin robe.

"What up wit' it, G-ma?"

"Hey, baby. How you doin'? You miss yo' G-ma?" asked Shenida with open arms.

"I'm just coolin, G-ma. You know I miss you," stated Khafre, hugging Shenida. "Who stay here?"

"This used to be your father's duck off spot."

"So it's yours now?" asked Khafre while following Shenida into the apartment.

"Nah, it's yours."

"What'chu mean?"

"Yo' father called and told me to give it to you for your birthday."

"My birthday been passed, G-ma."

"It's a belated gift. I got somethin' else for you too." Shenida smiled.

"Where it at?" asked Khafre, looking around.

"Go look in da room and get it off da bed." Excited to see what awaited him, Khafre went to the back room and came to an abrupt halt when he saw what laid on the bed for him.

"G-ma!" yelled Khafre, excited and confused all at once.

"Yeah, baby!"

"Dis for me?"

"Is a pig's pussy pork?"

"Gawwwwd! Thank you, G-ma!" Shenida slid her arms around Khafre from behind.

"You welcome," Shenida whispered in Khafre's ear before kissing him on the cheek. "Now, get in there," stated Shenida, pushing Khafre towards the bed. "Condom's in the dresser. I'll be out here if you need me." Shenida had paid an Instagram model to service Khafre for his birthday. She was an African beauty from Nigeria with a body so righteous that it gave you incentive to believe in God. Her skin was midnight-black and blemish-free, making her melanin glitter like gold.

"Join me, Khafre," Neema insisted, patting the open space next to her. Khafre removed his pistol and sat it on the dresser. He then removed his clothes and climbed in bed next to Neema.

"I love your accent," admitted Khafre.

"I believe I have a few more things you're going to love," Neema said, rubbing and kissing on Khafre's chiseled chest.

"Tell me, how do you want it?" added Neema between kisses.

"Do you, ma," replied Khafre, biting his bottom lip. Neema made her way to Khafre's nipple, ran her tongue across it, blew softly then began to suck it while she stroked his manhood. Khafre moaned with mixed feelings, not knowing if he should feel violated or turned on by what was occurring. In his mind only a woman's nipples were supposed to be kissed, licked, and sucked, but here was this grown African beauty instilling pleasures in him he never new existed. Neema was gentle, tender, and patient with every inch of Khafre's frame, confusing him all the more. *If Neema is just a gift then why is she tending to my body in a way that is consistent with making love?* Khafre thought. Whatever it was, Khafre was complying fully. He rubbed his hands through Neema's long natural, black silky hair as she made her way to his belly button, twirling her tongue in and around it.

"You like that?" questioned Neema as she made her way to Khafre's inner thighs and began to suck and kiss on them passionately while she stroked Khafre's shaft to a tender rhythm.

"Ssss—hell yeah," moaned Khafre, whining his hips with anticipation. Neema placed kisses on the head of Khafre's dick then ran her lips up and down the side of Khafre's shaft like a harmonica while massaging his balls. Just when the teasing was on the verge of driving Khafre crazy, Neema put every inch of him in her mouth and went to work. The pleasure was so intense that Khafre's toes curled and cracked as he attempted to crawl up the bed.

"Ssshhhhiiiit!" yelled Khafre, clutching the sheets as he began to shake and groan almost as if it were a cry for help. Neema moaned, sucked, and slurped like she was possessed by sex demons.

"Sss—shit! Arrrrrrrrhggg! Fuck!" moaned Khafre as he came in Neema's mouth. Neema continued to moan as she massaged Khafre's balls and sucked everything out of him. Neema's head skill was so intense that Khafre didn't go soft after coming. Neema reached n the dresser, grabbed a condom and put it on Khafre with her mouth.

"Damn, girl!" said Khafre, rubbing his hands through Neema's hair.

"What?" asked Neema while making her way back up Khafre's chest, leaving a trail of kisses. When she was eye to eye with Khafre, he grabbed her by her neck and looked deep into her eyes.

"You so fuckin' beautiful," said Khafre.

"Thank you," replied Neema then kissed Khafre deeply while mounting him.

"Sssss—oooh! Daddy, you feel good inside of me," moaned Neema as she rode Khafre slowly. She lifted to the tip of Khafre's dick, rotated her hips then slid back down all the while contracting her pussy muscles. Neema's pussy was so wet and tight that it sent chills throughout Khafre's body. As Neema continued to ride Khafre into bliss, he felt this warm sensational suction on his balls.

When Khafre leaned to get a glance around Neema, he saw Shenida sucking on his balls. Once again, he was confused and aroused. He didn't want to tell her to stop, but he had to ask her what was going on.

"G-ma?"

"Relax. Lay back and enjoy dis shit," instructed Shenida, pushing Neema forward, letting her know to sit on Khafre's face. Khafre saw that Neema's pussy was perfectly waxed, pretty and meaty. His mouth watered with anticipation, wrapping his arms around her succulent thighs as she straddled his face. Khafre wasted no time latching on her clit. The taste and aroma of her love flower sent blood rushing to Khafre's dick, making it the hardest erection he'd ever had. Neema moaned and gyrated her hips while Shenida eased down on every inch of Khafre in reverse cowgirl style.

"Umm—sss—shit! Ride that dick," moaned Khafre, then he continued to eat Neema out.

"Whoooooo—Shit! Sss—Shit, baby, damn!" groaned Shenida, her titties bouncing wildly as she rode Khafre like an equestrian.

"Yesss! Sss—eat this pussy, daddy, just like—sss—shit! I'm about to—sss—haooah, my God I'm, cum—sss—I'm coming, daddy," Neema cried, clenching her ass cheeks and rotating her pussy on Khafre's face, releasing her juices. Khafre devoured it all.

"Oooooowwwweeee—yes—sss—um skeetin' on dis dick, Khafre, damn!" yelled Shenida, shaking uncontrollably. Neema unstraddled Khafre's face, pushed Shenida forward and sucked her juices off of Khafre's dick. Khafre saw that Shenida was now face down, with her ass up. The arch in her back galvanized every inch of his flesh.

"Damn, G-ma!" Khafre stated with a glint in his eyes.

"Come get it," enticed Shenida, waving her perfect size ass as her pussy sat in place so elegantly from the back like a star fruit. Khafre took his dick out of Neema's mouth and made his way over to Shenida. He removed the condom and entered her slowly, grabbing her cotton-soft ass cheeks. They both moaned in ecstasy while Neema kissed Shenida down her back. When she reached Shenida's ass, she inserted her tongue and tongue-fucked her ass in rhythm opposite of Khafre's stroking of the vagina. Shenida's pussy creamed all over Khafre and smacked like milk poured over a bowl of *Rice Krispies*. Khafre grabbed Neema by her hair, removed his dick from Shenida and pushed it in Neema's mouth, then back in Shenida's pussy. He did this repeatedly until he came in Neema's mouth. Dying to get back into Neema's African pussy, Khafre pulled her to the edge of the bed, put Neema's thighs on his forearms and entered gently, stroking at a mild pace. Shenida sat her pussy above Neema's face.

"Stick yo' tongue out," demanded Shenida. Neema obeyed. Shenida lowered her clit on Neema's tongue and began to twerk at a steady pace. Seeing Shenida's ass jiggle gracefully as she looked back at him, Khafre went in beast mode. The sounds of both women moaning in bliss was too much to bear. Khafre grew two inches longer as he pounded between Neema's thighs and came powerfully. Neema screamed and squirted on Khafre's lower stomach simultaneously with Shenida creaming over her face. Khafre growled as he finished releasing himself in Neema then crashed on the bed, exhausted. Neema and Shenida did the same. Thirty minutes later when Khafre awoke, Neema was gone and Shenida laid wide awake smoking a blunt of sour disel.

"What up, G-ma?" asked Khafre groggily.

"Just up, thinkin' and shit," replied Shenida passing the blunt to Khafre.

"About?" asked Khafre, pulling from the blunt.

"I'm all over da place wit' it," admitted Shenida.

"Bidness?" asked Khafre, concerned.

"Yeah, that and some more shit."

"Whatever you need me fa, I'm here for it," said Khafre.

"I know, baby."

"I appreciate, that gift. I'll never forget it," Khafre stated with gratitude.

"Anythang for my baby. I see how you be lookin' at me, too, so—yeah, I blessed you."

"So, what now?" questioned Khafre.

100

"Look, I know you fuckin' Nilya and that's cool. What we did today was just a gift. A token of my appreciation for your loyalty. Dis shit stays between us. You hear me?"

"I hear you, G-ma," assured Khafre, passing her the blunt back.

"Okay. I love you, boy."

"I love you too, G-ma. I got some shit I need you to hear. I want yo' opinion."

"Run it," said Shenida, blowing smoke out of her nose. Khafre grabbed his phone and played the recorder. When the recorder stopped, Shenida sat up with an exasperated expression on her face. "That's dem niggaz you been running wit'?"

"Yeah, Quay and Reese," affirmed Khafre, his voice ringing with loathe. He was semi embarrassed that he had let them play up under him.

"You gotta move out here alone, kuz niggaz gon' snake you. You not like dem, Khafre, you cut different. I know what'chu gotta do. When you eradicate that problem, call me. I got the rest."

"A'ight, G-ma," said Khafre.

Khufu

Chapter Nineteen

It's Done

Khafre pulled into Sable Chase's apartment complex and dialed Reese's number. He answered on the third ring.

"What's good, my guy?" asked Reese excitedly.

"I'm callin' to see if y'all boys ready."

"Ready for what?" questioned Reese, already knowing why Khafre was calling.

"I got that for y'all."

"Say no more. Where you at?"

"I'm outside, y'all tighten' up!" ordered Khafre.

"We comin'now."

"Aye, Reese."

"Yeah."

"Task force out, heavy! Y'all leave dem pistols," Khafre advised.

"Oh yeah?"

"Yeah, I'm mad I had to leave my shit," lied Khafre.

"A'ight, we on our way down, bra." Reese hung the phone up. Moments later, Quay and Reese descended the steps, made their way over to Khafre's truck and got in.

"What's up wit' it, bossman?" asked Reese sarcastically with a smirk on his face.

"Yoooh! What's good?" asked Quay.

"Coolin', slow motion," replied Khafre, putting the truck in gear and pulling off.

"I hear that," said Quay.

"Y'all niggaz hungry? Y'all wanna stop somewhere and break bread?" asked Khafre.

"Hell yeah, fool, I'm hungry as fuck!" stated Reese. Quay slapped Reese in the back of the head.

"Nigga, you just ate some *Captain Crunch*! Let's go handle dis bidness first, greedy ass nigga."

"I'm straight, bra," said Reese.

"A'ight, shid—we can go somewhere later," assured Khafre. He turned the music up and vibed all the way out until he reached his new apartment.

"Why we in the back of the Brown Store?" questioned Reese.

"Dis my new spot. Come on, y'all, get out," instructed Khafre, hopping out of his truck. Quay and Reese followed suit. When they entered the apartment, Quay couldn't hide the malice in his heart when he saw that everything was designer from the carpet to the drapes.

"Damn. Versace everything, huh?" Quay stated with disdain.

"Yeah, Nilya decorated dis shit. I'on care nothin' bout dis shit," replied Khafre with nonchalance.

"I'm feelin' dis, fool." Reese said.

"You and Nilya exclusive now?" questioned Quay.

"Da shit in here," stated Khafre, ignoring Quay's interest. When Reese and Quay entered Khafre's bedroom, they saw ten bricks of fake molly and thirty thousand dollars on the bed.

"Grab that Louis bag out that closet, and put dem bricks in it," instructed Khafre.

"All of 'em?" asked Reese.

"Yeah. Ain't no rush though, take ya time," stated Khafre as his phone rang.

"Yah, what's up?" Khafre asked Nilya as he walked over to the window and took a quick glance out of it. Quay looked at Reese with raised eyebrows and nodded towards the money on the bed. Reese shook his head by way of saying: *No.*

"Yeah, I'll take you to da mall. You gotta buy me dem new Jordans though," exclaimed Khafre, chuckling. "A'ight, I'm on da way now." *Click!* Khafre hung up the phone.

"Y'all ready? I gotta go handle some shit. We can meet up later."

"Go, handle yo' bidness, fool. We'll hit'chu in a lil' bit," stated Reese, grabbing the Louis Vuitton bag and heading towards the front door with Quay behind him. Khafre took one last look at the money on the bed, and smirked. He then headed downstairs where

Quay and Reese awaited him. Once in the truck, Khafre fired up a blunt and pulled off.

"Since you got bidness to handle, you can drop us off at my auntie house, on Avenue Q," said Reese.

"It ain't a problem. I can take y'all to Sable Chase," Khafre assured.

"Nah. She wanted me to cut her grass, anyway," lied Reese.

"A'ight, say no more. Y'all wanna hit dis shit?" asked Khafre, attempting to pass the blunt to Reese.

"I'm cool," said Reese.

"Shid—let me hit it," Quay stated, reaching for the blunt.

"Where exactly on Avenue Q?"

"Pull in right there, behind that orange oldsmobile," replied Reese. Khafre complied.

"A'ight, bra, catch you later," said Reese, dapping Khafre up before hopping out of the truck. Quay tried to pass the blunt back to Khafre.

"I'm good, my nigga, ride out."

"Bet that up! You a solid nigga, Khafre," Quay stated before exiting the truck. Khafre blew the horn and pulled off.

***

"Hurry up, nigga, before dis green ass nigga come back," Quay whispered aggressively.

"Shut da fuck up, nigga, I got it," replied Reese through clenched teeth. Moments later, Reese finally jimmied the door open. They both rushed inside, adrenaline pumping on one-thousand. "I told you, nigga, I do dis shit," boasted Reese as they made their way to Khafre's bedroom.

"Damn, dis nigga sweet as fuck! He just left the money on the bed like that?" said Quay.

"Just hurry up and load da shit in da bag," ordered Reese.

"Damn! Y'all ain't gon' leave me nothin?" asked Khafre with two Rugers pointed at his supposed homeboys. Quay reached for his pistol but instantly remembered he'd left it at home.

"Nigga, did you just reach fo' ya bliky? Dis ain't no fuckin' movie, nigga!"

"Aye, man, whatever! Do you, homie!" Quay stated arrogantly.

"I already knew you was gon' say some gangsta shit before I send you into transition. But it's all good, baby, I'm here for it. And Reese, I'm disappointed in you. You broke my heart. You let dis nigga trick you out'cha life, bra." Reese said nothing. He knew he had betrayed a thorough nigga. He stood trembling with the anticipation of death.

"Nigga, spare all that philosophy shit. Fuck you think you is? Socrates or some shit!" said Quay. Khafre just laughed demonically.

"Nilya!" called Khafre. Seconds later, Nilya entered the room in all black, in a tight fitted hoodie, spandex pants and black boots. Khafre handed Nilya one of the Rugers.

"Well, ain't dis shit cute! You know what'chu doin', girl?" asked Quay with a smirk on his face. *Boc!* Nilya put one in Reese's head, causing blood and brain fragments to spray about Quay's face and mouth.

"Ahhh!" yelled Quay, frantically wiping the blood from his face." You crazy bitch! You killed my fuckin' cousin! Reese!" cried Quay, rubbing his hands through his dreadlocks. Khafre wasn't worried about Wolly in the store downstairs. Shenida had already paid him to hear nothing.

"You talk too damn much," stated Nilya.

"Hand me yo' gun, grab them zip ties and tie his hands," demanded Khafre. Nilya followed instructions, and Quay put up no resistance. After watching his cousin die, he had no more fight in him. "Brang his ass in here and sit 'em in dis chair in the bathroom." When Quay entered the bathroom, he noticed that a circle was cut out of the chair. Once he was seated, Khafre made Nilya zip-tie Quay's legs then grab a rope from under the bathroom sink to tie his body to the chair.

"You ain'tgotta do all dis shit, bra, just kill me!" whined Quay. Khafre ignored him and headed to the kitchen. He grabbed a bottle of honey and a cage from up under the kitchen sink, then headed back to the bathroom.

"Pull that nigga pants down and put dis on 'em. Make sure you rub plenty on his ass," ordered Khafre.

"What type of freak shit you on, man!" yelled Quay. Khafre stood silently as Nilya poured honey all over Quay's face, chest, and ass cheeks.

"A'ight, I got it from here. Wait for me outside." Before leaving, Nilya spat in Quay's face.

"Judas ass nigga!" Nilya stated before leaving.

"I'ma be honest wit'chu. I never liked you anyway, nigga! I'm glad you betrayed me. You just gave me motive."

"Nigga, fuck you!" yelled Quay.

"Yeah, I know it," replied Khafre, reaching for the cage. He then sat it in the bathroom, opened the cage and shut the door. Khafre had just released two possums in the bathroom. Quay could be heard screaming for his mother in a frenzy. Khafre commanded *Apple's* Alexa to play Plies' *Kept It Too Real* on his surround sound system and left the apartment. Two days later when he returned, all that was left of Quay were his bones. The possums were twice their size. Khafre called Shenida.

"Hello?' answered Shenida.

"G-ma, it's done."

"Say no more. I'm sending somebody to clean house right now. Leave the money on the bed."

"A'ight."

"Love you, boy."

"Love you too, G-ma."

Khufu

Chapter Twenty

You So Fuckin' Evil

After killing Quay and Reese, Khafre felt as if he was breathing air of a richer kind. It baffled him that their betrayal had no merit to it. It would be a while before he emanated his trust again. Khafre was staying at Shenida's house until Baby Haitian finished the clean up. He laid in Nilya's bed in a semi-conscious daydream until she rolled over and straddled him, bringing him back to reality.

"What'chu thinkin' about, Khafre," asked Nilya, rubbing on Khafre's chest.

"I'm just thinkin' 'bout how big dem possums was, after they ate that nigga Quay ass up. The only thang left was that nigga bones and shit," replied Khafre with a look of incredulity.

"What made you use them possums?"

"I read up on how they eat their prey ass first. Since Quay was always talkin' outta his ass, I figured that would be a proficient way to facilitate his demise."

"Proficient? Facilitate? You just so intellectual!"

"Man—fuck all that. I'm still trippin' on how you sprayed that nigga Reese brains all over Quay's face like you been killin' and shit. What that be 'bout?" Nilya inhaled and exhaled before replying.

"Khafre, you my best friend. Nigga, I've loved you since we we were snotty noses running the streets. You so fuckin' loyal and genuine. I guess when them niggaz betrayed you, a part of me felt betrayed too. So, fuck it, I'm ridin' wit'chu." Nilya leaned down, placing a wet kiss on Khafre's lips.

"I'm most definitely feelin' that," Khafre said fervently.

"Khafre," said Nilya, placing another kiss on Khafre's lips.

"Talk to me."

"I think we should be exclusive."

"What'chu mean?" asked Khafre.

"Nigga, don't play wit' me. You know what I mean! We should be together." A long blistering minute passed.

Khufu

"I'on know bout all that," replied Khafre as a flashback of Shenida riding him reverse cowgirl flashed through his mind.

"What da hell you mean you don't know?" questioned Nilya, seethingly.

"I mean, I kinda like it how we got it."

"I know you love me!" replied Niya.

"Of course."

"You ain't gon' find another bitch like me, Khafre."

"I know."

"Then what's the problem?" cried Nilya.

"Let me think about it, a'ight?"

"You promise you gon' think about it?" whined Nilya, grinding slowly on Khafre. Khafre rubbed his hands down Nilya's back and gripped her velvety ass cheeks.

"Shid—I'm thinkin' 'bout it right now!" said Khafre, grinding his manhood against Nilya's warm pussy.

"Let me help wit' that," Nilya stated, reaching for Khafre's dick with the intent of placing it deep inside her when Khafre's phone rang.

"Don't answer, baby," whined Nilya as she wiggled down on all of Khafre.

"Shiiit! Sss—damn! I got to hold on," said Khafre, grabbing his phone from the dresser.

"Yeah! Wassup?"

"Khafre!"

"Yeah, G-ma?"

"I need you to—"

"Shit!" moaned Khafre as Nilya sucked the head of his dick, which she'd already whipped out of his pants as he began talking to Shenida.

"You okay over there?" asked Shenida.

"I'm good, wassup, G-ma?" Khafre was trying hard to muffle his sounds of bliss.

"I need you to do somethin' for me."

"Drop the addy. I'm on the way."

"Okay, baby, I'll be waiting. Come now."

"I'm on it."

Shenida hung up. Before leaving, Khafre got a quickie. He didn't even bother to shower or wipe off. He just got in the wind.

***

It was a nice balmy afternoon at *Patty's Seafood*. Shenida was backed in at the restaurant, smoking a blunt of sativa with G-Baby's stepfather—D-Dog. Ever since G-Baby's incarceration, Shenida had been lounging at *Patty's Seafood*, catching plays. At the end of each day, Shenida would break D-Dog off for allowing her to hustle in the parking lot.

"When you gon' brang Khafre up here to see his grandma?" asked D-Dog, exhaling weed smoke.

"We ain't seen him since G-Baby got indicted," added D-Dog.

"As soon as I leave from up here, I'ma let 'em know y'all wanna see him," stated Shenida.

"Don't forget, Shenida. And the next time you hear from G-Baby, tell 'em I love him and he should keep his head up. I gotta get back in here, traffic pickin' up," exclaimed D-Dog, passing the blunt back to Shenida before heading inside the restaurant.

"I got'cha!" yelled Shenida. Moments later, an oldsmobile with a burgundy rag top pulled in front of Shenida's truck. Out of instinct, she reached under her seat for her pistol but realized she'd left it home because task force was beating the block heavy. Dipped in gold and black designer attire, Ponyboy hopped out of the oldsmobileand approached Shenida. Shenida opened her door and placed one foot out.

"Ponyboy, what's good?" asked Shenida, mentally download-ing Ponyboy's movement.

"Ain't nothin' you already know. Another day at it—slow mo-tion. Tell me somethin' good." Ponyboy rubbed his hands together.

"What'chu need?"

"Five bricks of molly."

"Fifty-bandz."

"Fifty-bandz? You done lost yo' ma'ami mind! G-Baby let me get'em for five! You charging me fuck nigga feez!" Ponyboy stated aggressively.

"Calm down, lil' nigga. Bring that shit down a notch. G-Baby ain't here right now. I got it. Now, my shit go for ten. If you ain't tryna grab nothin', you need to get da fuck outta here before you make things hot for yourself wit' all that po nigga shit. Task force already swangin' heavy!" noted Shenida.

"Po nigga shit? Hoe, you trippin!" Ponyboy snapped.

"I'll be a hoe. Da hoe wit' that work!" replied Shenida, smirking.

"Man, get dem five bricks up. I'm finna got to the car and get dis bag on yo' ass, hoe!" Ponyboy stated, walking off to go get the money. Shenida put five bricks in a brown bag and placed it on the passenger's seat. Moments later, Ponyboy returned with a Chanel bag.

"I keep money. Fuck you talkin' 'bout? Where that work at?" asked Ponyboy, unzipping his bag.

"Right here," replied Shenida, reaching for the brown bag. When she turned around, Ponyboy had a FN 9mm pointed at her face.

"You know what it is, hoe!" Ponyboy stated, showing all thirty-two gold teeth.

"Dis what we doing?" questioned Shenida in a molly tone, smiling.

"Why not? Shid—You tried me, hoe! Everytime I catch you up here, dis what it is!"

"Oh, okay. You got that, lil' daddy," said Shenida, handing Ponyboy the five bricks.

"Next time put some respect on my drip, hoe!" exclaimed Ponyboy before power-walking to his car and taking off. A '96 Toyota pulled out across the street from *Patty's Seafood* and blended in traffic, trailing Ponyboy. Ponyboy made his way down 23rd and made a right on 23rd and Avenue G. He then made a quick left into his driveway, hopped out with the brown bag and went into his house, leaving his car running. The Toyota pulled in front of Pony-boy's house and parked. Khafre hopped out with no mask and a .40 in hand. Ponyboy had left his door cracked, so Khafre slipped right in and heard rustling in a room to his left. When he entered the room, Ponyboy was so busy rumbling around in his closet that he never heard Khafre enter the house.

"Pussy ass hoe tried me. Talkin' bout ten a piece. Yeah, a'ight, hoe—got'cha dumb ass," muttered Ponyboy to himself. *Boc!* A hollow tip tunneled through the back of Ponyboy's head, spraying blood and brain matter all over the brown bag, killing him instantly. Khafre removed all Ponyboy's jewelry, grabbed the brown bag then took off. When Khafre backed in the driveway of an abandoned house across the street from *Patty's Seafood*, Shenida was still sitting in her truck. Khafre grabbed the blood-stained bag, hopped out of the Toyota and made his way across the street to Shenida's truck. He opened the passenger's side door, got in and handed the bag to Shenida. Her observation of the bag solidified what she already knew.

"Anybody see you?" asked Shenida.

"I doubt it. If they did, they know better," stated Khafre assuringly. Shenida gazed at Khafre with all kinds of thought in mind.

"What's good, G-ma?"

"Nothin'," replied Shenida, putting the truck in gear and pulling off. Ten minutes later they pulled up to a section at Taylor's Creek where people fished next to the waterfall. Unbeknownst to Shenida and Khafre, this was the same place that CC killed Yona.

"Come on, get out," instructed Shenida, grabbing a blunt before exiting her truck. Khafre got out and followed behind Shenida, enjoying the way her ass moved to an amusing rhythm. Shenida led him to a pier next to a waterfall and lit the blunt.

"Where we at?" asked Khafre.

"Taylor's Creek. I come here to clear my head sometimes," exclaimed Shenida, handing the blunt to Khafre.

"Dis shit look creepy as fuck," Khafre mentioned, looking around.

"I know, right. I guess that's why I like it," Shenida said, baring an insinuating smile.

"Look, Khafre, I appreciate 'chu holdin' me down. That shit mean everything to me."

"It ain't nothin', G-ma. You been there for me since my father left."

"I love you, boy," expressed Shenida, dropping to her knees and pulling Khafre's dick from his sweats.

"Hold up, G-ma!" enunciated Khafre, trying to warn Shenida that he had just pulled his dick out of her daughter, but he wasn't telling her nothing she didn't already know. Shenida smelled Khafre's dick, looked up at him and inserted him in her mouth whole. Her mouth was so warm with a vice-like grip that Khafre's knees buckled.

"Sss—damn, G-ma," moaned Khafre. Shenida grabbed him behind his knees and sucked his dick with no hands. She sucked, slurped, and moaned all the while looking up at Khafre as she put all of him in her mouth each time she bobbed up and down, driving Khafre crazy.

"Ssshit! You so fuckin' evil!"

Chapter Twenty-One

What's Next?

Aaron watched the door while G-Baby used the Allen key that he'd purchased from an inmate that worked with maintenance to remove the screws from the light where he kept his phone hidden. Once the phone was removed, G-Baby put the screws back in and took a seat on his bunk.

"Go 'head, bitch, I got'cha," assured Aaron. G-Baby dialed Khafre's number.

"Yeah! Who dis?" asked Khafre.

"You ain't got my number locked in? Di ya father."

"Oh, wassup, pops? Why you ain't been callin' me?"

"I been in here movin' around and shit. How you think you get that new truck?" asked G-Baby, smiling.

"You got that for me? I thought G-ma got it for me."

"Nah, that was my work. You like your new apartment?"

"Yeah! It's everythang to me, pops. Thank you, man, I love you."

"Anythang for my young king. You enjoyed that belated gift Shenida gave you?" Khafre grew silent as his heart rate accelerated. He knew that Shenida and his father were more than just business partners. The last thing he wanted was for his father to view him as being disloyal. "You still there?" asked G-Baby.

"Yeah, pops, I'm here," Khafre replied nervously.

"Look! It ain't nothin' I'on know, Khafre. That Nigerian Insta-gram model—I set that up. Even if I didn't set that up, I'll never have malice in my heart for another man 'bout a woman. Especially my son. You hear me?"

Khafre cleared his throat before speaking.

"Yeah, pops, I hear you."

"So, did yo' enjoy yo'self?"

"Hell yeah! I mean—yes, sir."

G-Baby laughed.

"You good. You ain't gotta censor yo'self when you talkin' to me. Just don't disrespect me."

"Yes, sir."

"You remember what I told you 'bout lovin' shit that makes you work?"

"Yes, sir."

"A'igh't. Don't let that shit wit' Shenida make you lose focus. I know that pussy and head smoking, but that's all it is. Momentary pleasure. You understand that?"

"I hear you, pops, and I love you for keepin' it so real wit' me."

"Always! I love you too, son. Listen. If I'm hearing yo' name in here, I know dem crackaz watchin' you. Just be careful, ya hear me?"

"I got'cha."

"One more thang. I talked to my lawyer, shit looking good on my appeal. Don't tell nobody though. I wanna just pop up on some shit."

"I can't wait till you come home, man."

"Look, I gotta go. Love you son."

"Love you too, pops." After hanging up the phone G-Baby put the phone back in the light.

"Everythang a'ight wit'cha?" asked Aaron.

"Yeah, man, my son growin' up fast and shit."

"You'll be back out there in a minute, just chill. He gon' be a'ight."

"Man, they gotta kill me next time, bra," said G-Baby, shaking his head.

"You too?" replied Aaron sardonically. "You wanna drink?" asked Aaron.

"Hell yeah."

"Go down there and get it from Sleepy. I already paid for it."

"A'ight," said G-Baby, leaving the room. When G-Baby made it to Sleepy's room, he found Sleepy standing in front of his cell agitated.

"What up wit' it, Sleepy?" asked G-Baby.

"Man, my cellie been in the room for thirty minutes with the flap up. This nigga trippin'."

"He probably constipated—or dead," stated G-Baby jokingly. "Aaron sent me at that drink."

"Man—fuck this shit!" proclaimed Sleepy, snatching the cell door open.

"Woooeee!" muttered G-Baby.

"Da fuck!" yelled Sleepy. What was being seen would be talked about for years to come. Sleepy's cellie had a mirror on the door, jacking off to his own ass. He now stood in the cell embarrassed and naked.

"Nigga, what da fuck is you on?" Sleepy asked Ben.

"Man, man, I'm just tired of jackin' off to pictures, man. I need somethin' real," cried Ben.

"Nigga! Ya own—don't worry bout it. Hand me that bottle outta my locker," demanded Sleepy. Ben went in Sleepy's locker and threw him the bottle of white lighting, while attempting to cover himself with his other hand. "Here." Sleepy handed G-Baby the bottle, pulled his knife and went in the cell, closing the door behind him. G-Baby could hear Ben wailing and calling for help as he headed back up the steps. Before heading in his room, he heard Ben busting out of the room yelling for the office. When G-Baby looked up, Ben was dripping in blood completely naked and running to the officers' station. G-Baby went in his room and climbed in his bunk.

"What's all that noise out there?" asked Aaron, putting down a book that he was reading.

"Sleepy just poked Ben up," said G-Baby.

"For what?"

'Grab you a cup. You gon' need a drink for dis one." Seconds later, the duces could be heard going off. Moments after that, the goon squad rushed in the dorm.

"Lock down! Get to your fucking cell! Lock Down!"

***

"Who was that on the phone?" asked Nilya.

"My father," replied Khafre, making a left on 29th and Avenue Q.

"What was y'all talkin' about?"

"Touch ya nose."

"Why you ain't tell him about us?"

"The same reason you ain't tell Dirk."

"I'ma tell Dirk!" said Nilya, lips tightening with resolution.

"Take ya time. Ain't no rush."

"Whatever, lil' head."

"You hungry?" asked Khafre.

"Yeah, I want Rice Hut," replied Nilya in a child-like voice.

"You know dem people serving cats, and you still eatin' that shit. That's crazy!" exclaimed Khafre, making a left on 29th and Avenue D.

"If cat taste that good, keep it comin' baby," stated Nilya, her face crinkled in laughter.

"That shit ain't funny, it's sad," asserted Khafre, shaking his head as they pulled into the Chinese Rice Hut on 25th and Avenue D. Khafre hopped out in his red hooded sweat suit and waved Nilya out of the truck. Nilya saw that Khafre left his gun in the middle console, so she grabbed it, tucked it in her matching hooded sweat suit and got out of the truck.

"I'm comin', boy, dang!" said Nilya.

"Da hell you was doin' in there stealin'?" joked Khafre, putting his arm around Nilya's neck.

"Yep. All ya lil' pocket change."

"You a trip. You know I love you, right?" asked Khafre.

"I know that since we were little when you killed that dog for me."

"You remember that?" said Khafre, opening the door for Nilya.

"Never forget it," replied Nilya, stopping to kiss Khafre passionately.

"A'ight now, bend ya ass over one of deez tables in here." Nilya ran to a table, bent over and started twerking while looking back at Khafre.

"Come get it then, tough ass nigga," dared Nilya.

"Girl, come order yo' food before you fuck 'round and give dis old ass Chinaman a heart attack throwin' all that ass like that."

"Boy, please! I know he gotta brothel full of china ass some-where. Mr. Chinaman, tell him you done seen plenty of ass before."

"Place order please!" said the Chinaman, his voice ringing with irritation.

"Okay, I'ma need you to calm down. Once you do that, let me get twenty piece all flats and some fried rice wit' extra eggs.

"Sauce?"

"Honey mustard. Khafre, what'chu want?" asked Nilya.

"I'm good," replied Khafre, going through his phone as he sat at a table. While Nilya was paying for her order, a youngin' by the name of Papa George entered the Rice Hut and stood behind Nilya.

"Let me get one of them Mistic's too," said Nilya.

"Eleven dolla!" replied the Chinaman, handing Nilya a ticket. For some strange reason, Papa George kept staring at Khafre with a screw face.

"Nigga, you a'ight?" asked Khafre aggressively.

"It depends, nigga!" replied Papa George aggressively.

"Nigga, spare me da enigma, wassup?" asked Khafre, looking around the small building to see if it had cameras.

"Where da fuck you get that jewelry from?" asked Papa George.

"I got it where I got it, nigga. What's next?"

"That look like my lil' brother shit, nigga!" Papa George stated, pulling his pistol. Khafre sat unnerved because he'd seen Nilya cuff his pistol before getting out of his truck. In Khafre's mind Papa George was doing too much talking. He knew that Khafre was wear-ing his dead brother's jewelry and he hadn't started squeezing yet. He held his pistol at his side breathing and moving side to side er-ratically.

"I got it from Ponyboy, bitch ass nigga," taunted Khafre. Papa George attempted to raise his gun but it was too late. *Boc!* Nilya hit Papa George behind his ear, putting him in a transitional state in-stantly.

"Let's go put'cha hoodie on," ordered Khafre, grabbing Nilya by the hand. The Chinaman stayed low under the counter until Khafre and Nilya were gone. Bodies dropping at the Rice Hut was the norm in Fort Pierce. As soon as Papa George's body was removed from the property, business would resume as normal.

Chapter Twenty-Two

Promise Me

Shantel laid in her bed stolidly, watching an episode of *Power*, trying desperately to ignore Will and his crazy antics. He had been rambling and complaining about Shantel not being as affectionate as she used to.

"I'm trying to watch TV, man. Dang! Can you please go in the living room, wit' that shit!"

"Fuck you and that TV, hoe! I don't give a fuck 'bout what'chu tryin' to watch! Hoe, I'll break that TV. Fuck you mean!" yelled Will.

"What is your problem?" Shantel seethed.

"Bitch! You my fuckin' problem! I know you fuckin' somebody else! You damn sure ain't been giving it to me. Then when I try to touch you, you treat me like filth in dis bitch!"

"That should tell you something," Shantel replied nonchalantly. This pushed Will over the edge.

"Bitch, I'll break yo' fuckin' neck in here," threatened Will, throwing Shantel's crystal bird at her seventy-inch flat screen.

"Can you please leave now? Please just go. I done asked you nicely."

"You asked me nicely? Bitch, I ain't goin' no fuckin' where! How about that?" Shantel said nothing else. She calmly grabbed her phone and dialed out. "Who you callin'? You call in the law?" Shantel just smirked.

***

After throwing his pistol in Taylor's Creek, Khafre headed to his apartment to shower and get rid of his blood-tainted clothes. Shenida had remodeled the entire apartment with Armani after Baby Haitian cleaned the remains of Quay and Reese. Nilya fired question after question at Khafre as he dressed himself.

"You killed Ponyboy?" asked Nilya curiously.

"That bothers you?"

"No, nigga! I'm ridin' wit'chu. I'm just wondering why you ain't tell me. That lil' boy use' to try to holla at me. So why did you kill 'em?"

"Leave it alone, Nilya," exclaimed Khafre, slipping on his black Timberlands.

"Oh, it's one of dem, huh? You must have been wit' my mama when you killed him. That's the only time you be all secretive and shit. But'chu love me though." Nilya shook her head in disbelief. "You know you gotta be a different type of evil to wear a dead man's jewelry. Especially if you the one who killed him." Khafre continued to dress in silence. Nilya gazed at Khafre for a few terrifying seconds with piercing eyes.

"Khafre, did you fuck my mama?" Nilya asked, afraid of the answer.

"What kinda—" Khafre's phone rang.

"Fuck that phone, Khafre. Answer my question!" Nilya demanded.

"Hello? Yeah, ma. He did *what*? I'm on my way." Khafre hung up his phone, grabbed a gun from under his mattress and headed for the door. "Come on," demanded Khafre. Nilya sneered and did as she was told. Shantel stayed around the corner from the Brown Store, so Khafre was there in no time. Nilya stayed in the truck while Khafre hopped out gun in hand. He entered the house with murder on his mind.

"Mama! Where you at?"

"I'm back here!" said Shantel. When Khafre entered her room, he saw that her TV was destroyed.

"You a'ight, ma?"

"Yeah, I'm okay. He didn't hit me. I just wanted him to leave. I'm done wit' him," assured Shantel.

"Where he at?"

"He left when I told him I was callin' you," Shantel stated, getting up from her bed and wrapping her arms around Khafre's waist, burying her head in his chest. "I miss you so much."

"I miss you too, ma."

"I'm sorry I hurt'chu. I was just lonely. I miss your father so much," Shantel admitted as tears fell from her eyes.

"Don't trip, ma. It's all good. I overstand."

"Thank you for coming."

"Who would I be if I didn't? I see the nigga done broke ya TV. Here—" Khafre went in his pocket and handed Shantel a nice bank-roll. "Go get'chu another one."

"Thank you," replied Shantel, tucking the money in her jeans. "You hungry?"

"I'm good, ma."

"Okay. Boy, put that gun away." Khafre laughed and tucked the gun.

"Yes, ma'am."

"Have you spoke to your father?" asked Shantel, placing her hands on her hips.

"Yes, ma'am, I talked to him."

"How he doin'?"

"That's pops. You know he always good."

"Tell 'em to call me next time you hear from him."

"A'ight mama, I'm gone. I got Nilya out here in da truck. Call me if you need me."

"Okay. Tell Nilya I said, hey. Love you."

"Love you too, mama." Khafre headed back to his truck, feeling relieved that his mother was okay. When he hopped in his truck, Nilya was in a hysteric state. Her right leg was shaking as if she had bad nerves and tears fell from her face irresistibly.

"You a'ight?" Khafre asked. Nilya stopped shaking her leg, wiped her tears with the back of her hands and gazed at Khafre grimly. In one swift motion, Nilya snatched Khafre's gun from his pocket and pointed it at his face.

"You know better than that," Khafre stated, unmoved, starting his truck up.

"I know I'ma blow yo' shit off in front of yo' mama house if you dont' answer my fuckin' question! Did you fuck my mama? Yes or fuckin' no?" yelled Nilya, gun shaking

"If you got that gun in my face you obviously believe I fucked her. Do you."

"Answer the fuckin—" *Boc!* Nilya missed Khafre's face by an inch, putting a hole in his window. Khafre looked at the hole in his window, then back at Nilya menacingly who was now holding her hand over her mouth. "I'm sorr—" Khafre dropped the truck in gear pedal to the floor, causing Nilya's head to slam into the headrest. He then snatched the gun from her and placed it in his lap.

"Khafre, I'm sorry—I didn't mean it," cried Nilya. Khafre said nothing as he noticed red and blue lights in his rearview mirror.

"Fuck man! Now I gotta deal wit' dis shit!" stressed Khafre, gripping his pistol.

"What'chu gon' do?" questioned Nilya.

"Fuck you think I'ma do?" replied Khafre, his mind pregnant with ideas.

"You can't kill 'em, Khafre. He already turned his lights on. That means the camera on his dash is on. Give me the gun," Nilya advised, holding her hand out. "Hurry up!" Khafre handed Nilya the pistol, who quickly tucked it in her Birkin bag. "That ain't no city cop neither. It looks like a detective," stated Nilya. Khafre pulled over by the park on Avenue M by the projects. Detective Archie wasted no time hopping out of his unmarked vehicle. He approached Khafre's door and opened it.

"Step outta the fuckin' vehicle!" ordered Archie, with his weapon drawn.

"What's da problem, detective?" asked Khafre, hands in the air.

"Against the car, bitch ass nigga! Hands behind ya back! You so much as wiggle ya ears out this mothafucka, I'ma shoot da shit out'cha!" warned Archie. Khafre complied. Archie put away his weapon and cuffed Khafre. He then walked Khafre to the back of his unmarked car and placed his back against it, forcing Khafre to face him.

"What'chu fuckin' wit' me for?" asked Khafre.

"Nigga, you was swerving," replied Archie showing all thirty-two of his gold teeth. Archie was a street nigga turned cop. He wore jewelry and even had dreads. He went to school with Khafre's father—G-Baby.

"Well, give me my damn citation and let me roll out then, nigga."

"Shut the fuck up, nigga, fa I bust yo' head in front of deez projects, nigga." Khafre looked Archie square in his eyes, refusing to blink. He wanted Archie to see what laid behind his eyes. Archie knew Khafre was a killer, but was unfazed. Archie was a killer too. He'd killed six people, three on duty and three off duty. "How you get that bullet hole in yo' window?"

"When I jumped in my shit dis mornin' It was already there, detective."

"I smell bullshit. So why you killed Kurt?"

"I don't know what'chu speakin' of, detective."

"He was fuckin' ya lil' girlfriend, huh?"

"Imagine that," laughed Khafre.

"Yo' name been coming up in a lot of shit. What that be 'bout?"

"It's yo' job to find that shit out. Good luck wit' that." Khafre sounded cocky.

"Oh, I ain't tryin' to case you up. We way past that," Archie pronounced, drawing his weapon and pressing it to Khafre's temple. "I'ma put yo' lil' ass in a fuckin' box, so don't let me catch ya ass under the moon. Oh ya—tell yo' bitch ass daddy I know he had somethin' to do wit' my partner gettin' killed. He knows what it is," expressed Archie through clenched teeth.

"You a'ight, homie?" a voice behind Archie asked. When Archie turned his head to the side, he saw a young Puerto Rican—who everybody called Chico Sito—clutching a modified .40 caliber that contained an extended clip and green beam.

"Yeah, I'm good, bra," replied Khafre.

"Fuck that! I ain't movin' till dis fuck nigga leave!" Chico Sito stated. Archie holsted his weapon and uncuffed Khafre.

"I'ma see you later, lil' nigga. You too," said Archie, pointing at Chico.

"I ain't hidin', nigga! I'm right here in the projects. Look me up, nigga," said Chico with fire in his eyes. Archie smiled, hopped in his car and pulled off.

"Bet that up! Where you from, bra?" asked Khafre, impressed.

"I moved down here from Ocala, Florida. I stay in the projects wit' my baby mama," stated Chico. "I see you ain't like how da nigga was flexin'. What'chu an' him got goin' on?"

"Long story," said Khafre.

"I got time," exclaimed Chico.

"Later. Shoot me yo' number. We gon' link up."

"Definitely." Khafre logged Chico in his phone then hopped in his truck.

"You okay?" asked Nilya.

"So you was gon' let da nigga kill me, huh?" asked Khafre, pulling off.

"I was gon' get out but I saw that Puerto Rican boy step up, so I just stayed inside," Nilya proclaimed. Khafre shook his head in disbelief.

"That's a fuckin' lie! The Nilya I know woulda got out and assisted me. You let yo' emotions get in the way of what's important!"

"Yeah, and what is that?" asked Nilya, head tilted to the side.

"Preservation! Survival! A lil' loyalty woulda been nice!" said Khafre.

"Loyalty? Nigga, I just killed a man in a public place of bidness. I saved your fuckin' life!"

"I rather die at the hands of my own kind before a fuckin' cop! When we out here in the field, you leave yo' feelings at home, on the fuckin counter!"

"Tsss—whatever, Khafre, man. You say you love me but'chu can't even look me in my eyes when I ask you, is you fuckin' my mama. Payin' attention to detail is one of my most potent assets. If you really loved me, you would know that, Khafre." Tears welled up in Nilya's eyes and cascaded down her face.

"Fuck all that! You pullin' guns on me and shit. You coulda blew my fuckin' head off!   But'chu love me though."

"And you still can't answer my question."

"If you really feel like I'm fuckin' yo' mama, ask her."

"Where we do that at? My mama is like my best friend. I'll neva pull up on my mama over some dick. In life we only get one mama, but dick is plentiful. You know what? Drop me off. I'm ready to get the fuck away from you!" Nilya waved her hand dismissively and turned her back towards Khafre to gaze out of the window.

"That's wassup. Hand me my pistol."

"Tsss—" sighed Nilya, reaching in her purse to hand Khafre his gun. She handed him the gun, still gazing out of the window, refusing to look at him out of disappointment. All Nilya wanted was for Khafre to tell her that she was crazy and that he would never betray her. She wanted to know that she was everything to him like he was to her, but instead Khafre was acting odd. He loved Nilya dearly but he couldn't bring himself to tell her the truth, so combativeness was his only defense mechanism.

"You trippin," implied Khafre, placing the gun on his lap.

"Nigga, fuck you!"

"Come on, Nilya. You don't mean that," replied Khafre, pulling in front of Nilya's home.

"Look, don't call me, text me, none of that shit, Khafre, we over," declared Nilya, reaching for the door. Khafre grabbed her arm.

"Nilya, hold up, wait," pleaded Khafre.

"Man—what, Khafre?" asked Nilya, her eyes teary.

"Look, you know how I feel about'chu. I never lied to you about anything since day one. Not once and I never will."

"Khafre!"

"Nilya, hear me out," expressed Khafre with a casual tone of entitlement. Nilya relaxed and gave Khafre undivided attention.

"I'm listening."

"You know yo' mother been there for me since my father been gone. She showed me how to move out here and I love her for it. We have committed some vile acts together, and I regret none."

"*Vile*? Vile like what? What'chu mean?" questioned Nilya, baffled. Khafre exhaled before replying.

"We killed together for my birthday. We, ahh—"

A black unknown vehicle pulled along side of Khafre's truck, causing his words to be cut short. To Khafre's surprise, a woman popped out of the sunroof—gun in hand—and let off multiple shots. Khafre opened his door and slid out unscathed, rounded the back of his truck and returned fire, dropping the back window out but it was too late. The shooter had already pulled off with mission accomplished. Khafre rushed to Nilya's door that was riddled with bullet holes, and opened it. His body was instantly wrapped in a sheet of blazing terror when he saw Nilya choking, clutching her chest and chasing her breath.

"Nilya!" Khafre yelled, placing his hands on the holes in her chest. Nilya attempted to talk, coughing blood in Khafre's face.

"Kha—Khafre—I'm okay—right?" asked Nilya, coughing up more blood.

"Yeah, you good, big head, you gon' make it," Khafre affirmed, trying to keep Nilya conscious. He kissed her on her blood-saturated lips and closed the door. A numbness fanned through Khafre's body as he made his way around the truck, hopped in and floored it to the hospital. Khafre ran every light in sight as he called Lawnwood Medical Center to let them know that he was on the way.

"Nilya! Stay wit' me, bae. You know I need you! I love you! You hear me, Nilya? I love you!"

"I—lov—love you—to—too," replied Nilya, still struggling for air in her lungs.

"We almost there! You gon' make it! You hear me?"

"Pro—promise me—you—gon—kill 'em. Pro—promise me, Khafre."

"I promise! We gon' get 'em together!" Khafre assured, pulling into the hospital and heading to the back. When he pulled up, EMT's were already waiting with a stretcher. Khafre hopped out, barking orders at the EMTs frantically.

"Help her! She been shot!" EMT's rushed into action, pulling Nilya from the truck and on to the stretcher. Khafre was headed in the hospital when he realized he still had a gun on him and the police would be pulling up at any second. "Make sure she good!" yelled

Khafre, backpedaling to his truck. He got in and pulled off. Replaying the scene in his mind, the shooter could be seen clear as day. Khafre knew it was Saudia avenging her brother Kurt's death, but what he didn't know was that Nilya was already dead when EMT's pulled her from his truck.

Khufu

Chapter Twenty-Three

Death Is Easy

It was a soft summer day, the sun blazing down as the clouds floated without physical restriction. Nilya's popularity had the church—Greater New Bethel—filled to capacity. Divas, gangstas, nerds, old and young came out to pay their respect. The cars were parked all the way around the corner, some even blocking the driveways of people's homes. Nilya was dressed in a fifteen-hundred-dollar Loewe dress as she laid peacefully in a Versace casket. Shenida was clothed in a Jacquemus skirt, Brock's collection jacket, with an all-white Khaite coat. She had on Jessica McCormack earrings, rings by L'Enchanteur and Brent Neale, together with a Tiffany locket with Nilya's picture in it. Tears spilled down both sides of her face as she tried rigorously to subjugate the pain of losing her only child. Khafre sat next to Shenida in a Salvatore Ferragamo suit, occasionally wiping away her tears. He had yet to shed tears behind Nilya's death. The weight of the world fanned a numbness in his body from head to toe. Shenida tried desperately to convince Khafre that Nilya's death wasn't his fault, but he knew better. People were giving Shenida their condolences after viewing Nilya's body. Dirk, Nilya's boyfriend, approached her casket and kissed her on her cheek.

"I tried to warn you about that nigga. Now look at you. Look at what you got me going through, baby. It's all good though. I love you forever," whispered Dirk, kissing Nilya one more time before approaching Shenida to give his condolences.

"I'm sorry for your loss," expressed Dirk, grilling Khafre all the while. Khafre reached for his gun but Shenida grabbed his hand and shook her head. Dirk nodded warily before walking off, heading out of the church. When everybody was done viewing Nilya's body, Khafre got up and approached Nilya's casket. He couldn't believe how peaceful she looked in death.

"Hey, big head. You so beautiful I miss you. I love you." Khafre used his index finger to stroke Nilya's cheek. "You such a designer fiend, you had to be buried in a Versace casket. You so spoiled even in death," said Khafre, laughing to suppress his pain. He removed a Versace scarf from his pocket and laid it across her neck. After giving her a forehead kiss, Khafre pulled a blunt from his jacket pocket and lit it, causing people in the church to gasp and mumble disbelief. "I'ma smoke one wit'cha, one last time, big head," Khafre started blowing smoke in Nilya's face. Moments later, he felt an arm around his waist. It was Shenida.

"Let me hit it, Khafre," exclaimed Shenida, reaching for the blunt. By this time people were storming out of the church, disgusted with Khafre and Shenida's actions. The only people who remained were the pallbearers.

"You know yo' father once told me, *Death is easy*, and that *livin' is the hard part*. My baby at peace now. I don't want'chu to go about livin' yo' life with guilt and regret. We both know what comes with this life. You just make sure I'm not the only one cryin'. You hear me?" asked Shenida, blowing smoke from her nose.

"I hear you, and I feel you," Khafre assured.

"Okay, baby. Y'all go 'head, carry my baby outta here," instructed Shenida, passing Khafre the blunt. The pallbearers did as they were told. Khafre and Shenida walked ahead of the casket. When they made their way outside, Khafre made a left and stood on the corner, finishing the last of the blunt, while Shenida watched the pallbearers load Nilya into the hearst. All of a sudden, screeching tires could be heard coming up the street. When Khafre turned around, Dirk was hanging out the passenger's side of the car. Khafre drew his Desert Eagle. When the car made its way to the corner, Khafre could see that Saudia was the driver. When Dirk attempted to slip back in the car, Khafre let off every round he had, hitting Dirk in the head. He dropped the SK with half of his body slumped out of the sunroof, as Saudia drove recklessly away from the scene. Khafre ran over to the bullet-riddled hearst and saw that Shenida was lying on her back with a massive hole in her stomach. She tried desperately to put her organs back in her stomach but to no avail. Khafre cradled Shenida in his arms until she took her last breath. Shenida died with her eyes open.

Chapter Twenty-Four

Repent For Your Sins

Khafre laid blighted in his apartment as the afternoon sunlight bled through the windows of his bedroom. Losing two of his favorite people in tandem had him emotionally depleted. Dealing with another funeral would have been too arduous for Khafre to do, so he had Shenida cremated. Her ashes sat on a dresser next to Khafre's bed as he stared blankly at the ceiling while smoking a blunt. His phone rang, startling him a little.

"Yeah," said Khafre with pain filtering through his voice.

"How you holdin' up?" asked G-Baby.

"Dis shit hurt, pops. I'on wish dis shit on no man. Shit hurt like a muthafucka, pops!"

"I know but'chu gon' be a'ight," assured G-Baby.

"I'm not overstandin' why you ain't as pissed as me. You loved Shenida, pops."

"I'ma always love her, and receiving that news did drop some pain on me. But, I can't afford to lose focus in a war zone I'm currently in about a death out there. I gotta keep rollin' on. Ya hear me?"

"Yeah," stated Khafre dryly.

"You don't sound like you gon' recover from dis no time soon. I told you 'bout lovin' shit that makes you weak. Now look at'cha. Suffering is a price we pay for attachments. Right now, you feeling like all dis is yo' fault but guilt disappears wit' overstanding. Don't sit around and cry 'bout it, nigga. You know what'chu gotta do. Now, I just called to check on ya. I gotta lawyer visit, so I gotta go."

"Pop!"

"Yeah?"

"Mama say call her."

"She a'ight?"

"Yeah, you know I make sure of that."

"A'ight, I'ma call her. I love you, son."

"I love you too, pops." *Click!* G-Baby hung up. Khafre just laid there and pondered on everything his father had said.

***

It had been a good night at Bingo for Ms. Ionis. She had won five-hundred dollars and was now planning to go to Outback Steakhouse with Don, Kurt's friend. Don had been making sure Ms. Ionis was taken care of ever since Kurt's death. He'd been mowing her lawn, taking out her trash, and assisting her to Bingo every Friday night.

"You was on fire tonight, Ms. Ionis," exclaimed Don.

"I sure was, wasn't I? It's because I wore my lucky sweater tonight. My mother knitted this sweater for me before her passing."

"That's probably what it was. She was looking down on you."

"Umm—humm."

"I seen how them men was looking at'chu too. I think Mr. Freddy likes you." Don opened the car door for Ms. Ionis. Ms. Ionis stopped and stood by her car door before speaking.

"Chile, I ain't got time for no man right now." Before Don could reply, he saw Ms. Ionis's eyes grow in size. *Boc!* Sito put a hole in the back of Don's head, causing blood and brain matter to splatter about on Ms. Ionis's face, neck, and chest. She attempted to scream but Khafre quickly wrapped his arms around her neck from behind and dragged her to a stolen van that was parked next to her car. After securing her in the van, Sito pulled off, leaving Don next to Ms. Ionis's car with his brains left on the pavement for public display. Fifteen minutes later, Sito pulled up in the back of Shenida's home, got out and opened the door for Khafre. To Khafre's surprise, Ms. Ionis didn't put up any resistance. She complied fully and entered the house as if she were a guest. When Khafre looked back, Sito was standing out the door.

"What's good, bra?" asked Khafre.

"You go ahead and do you, homie.

"What'chu mean?"

"Wackin' niggaz ain't nothin', but kids and mamas and shit—I'm fuck off. Handle yo' bidness. I'ma get rid of the van."

"I overstand, Sito. Thanks for ya help, though. I'ma hit'chu later," Khafre stated, his arms still around Ms. Ionis's neck.

"Yeah," replied Sito, stepping out the door and closing it. Khafre guided Ms. Ionis to a chair in the kitchen and made her have a seat. He then grabbed the rope from the table and tied her to the chair.

"Who are you?" asked Ionis, perplexed. Khafre pulled a chair and sat in front of her.

"You don't know who I am?"

"I do not," Ionis stated matter-of-factly.

"I killed your son," asserted Khafre, looking her square in the eyes. Ms. Ionis didn't bat a lash. She looked Khafre in his eyes and smiled before replying.

"I already forgave you for that, baby. You see, the bible says I have to, in order to enter the kingdom of heaven. I can't let your actions hinder me from gettin' right with the Lord," Ionis stated sternly.

"Oh, you are one of them, huh?"

"How do you mean?" asked Ionis, confused.

"You are of them pie-in-the-sky types who believes in spookism," said Khafre, violently agitated.

"Call it what you want to, young man. You are entitled to an opinion. Now if you brought me here to kill me, you need to do what you got to do but don't disrespect my belief because I'm prepared to die for it," declared Ionis, her voice soft as snowfall.

"I'm not gon' kill you for your beliefs, but'chu will die for the sins of your daughter," Khafre stated icily. Ionis inhaled, exhaled, then held her head high, looking Khafre in his eyes.

"I'm prepared to do that," assured Ionis.

"I honor that," replied Khafre.

***

Two Weeks Later—

It was a smoggy afternoon, on a Friday. The projects was clustered with kids, some spraying each other with a water hose, while others begged their mother to buy them ice cream from the passing ice cream trucks. Saudia had to blow her horn to get the kids out of her driveway who were throwing mud pies.

"I can't stand deez bad ass kids," muttered Saudia through clenched teeth. She put her car in *park*, and got out. "Y'all got mud all on the side of my damn house! I should tear y'all ass up then make you go get'cha mama, so I can whoop her ass too!" yelled Saudia.

"Sorry, Miss Saudia," cried the four kids who were covered in mud.

"Sorry my ass! Get da hell outta my yard!" The kids dispersed as Saudia made her way to the front door, unlocked it and entered. When Saudia plopped down on her Goodwill sofa, she noticed that her TV was on. "I could have sworn I cut that damn TV off." Saudia shrugged, grabbed a half of blunt from the coffee table and lit it. When she exhaled and looked to her right, she saw bread and meat on the table along with a jar of mayo.

"Da fuck?" Saudia exclaimed, as she looked around questioningly. As soon as the words left her mouth, the word "play" was displayed on her TV screen. After squinting to focus on what was in front of her, it became apparent that the person sitting in a chair, reading bible scriptures from the King James Version was her mother.

"Mama?" said Saudia, confused as ever. Once Ionis was finished reading from the bible, she sat it down on a table next to her and looked deep into the camera.

"Saudia, baby, I love you."

"Love you too, ma," whispered Saudia, still confused.

"I would encourage you to go on and accomplish great things in life but that advice would be of no use. If my assumptions are correct, you should be passing over to the spiritual realm shortly, as will I."

"What'chu talkin' about?" asked Saudia, her voice loud as if her mother could hear her.

"Get right with God and repent for your sins. It's not too late. I love you and if you're watching this that means that I'm already dead." *Boc!* The sound of a gunshot resounded from the TV. Saudia flinched then put her hand over her mouth as tears instantly fell from her eyes.

"Mama?" cried Saudia, her hands quivering. Another figure stepped in front of the camera and leaned in so Saudia could get a clear view. Saudia gasped.

"Khafre?" I'ma fuckin' kill you, nigga! I swear on everything I love!" Saying nothing, Khafre disappeared from the screen, then returned holding a machete. He pointed it at the camera like a batter taunting a pitcher, hiked his left leg up and swung the machete with everything he had. Ms. Ionis's head came off and struck the camera, splattering blood on the lens.

"Aaahh! Oh my God!" screamed Saudia, falling into a traumatized state. Khafre slipped out of a closet behind her and tiptoed towards her. Spotting a glare in the TV, Saudia turned around only to be met by Khafre's Glock 19 fracturing her skull and knocking her out cold. When Saudia regained consciousness, she attempted to move but to no avail

When she looked up, she realized that she was naked and cuffed to her bedpost with her legs spreaded horizontally. A horrid sensation immediately wavered throughout her body as she thought of her fate. Moments later, Khafre entered the room, stood next to the bed and gazed at Saudia ominously. She tried to read Khafre's thoughts through his eyes but she saw nothing but a void and hollowness. At that very second, Saudia knew that this was her last day in the physical.

"You started this shit when you killed my brother, nigga! Then you had the nerve to come to his candle lighting and kill lil' Poo Poo! You got everythang you deserve, bitch ass nigga!" exclaimed Saudia, managing to spit in Khafre's face. Khafre said nothing. He bent down, grabbed Saudia's panties and wiped his face. He then grabbed a duct tape from the dresser, stuffed the panties in her mouth and taped it shut. On the side of Saudia's bed was a dresser where Khafre had his torture kit. He grabbed a pair of wire cutters, gripped Saudia's left breast and clipped her nipple off. Blood shot from her breast while the duct tape muffled her cries of agony. Khafre did the same to her right breast then grabbed a bottle of lemon juice and poured it where her nipples used to be. Saudia bucked but it was futile. Khafre made his way around the bed after grabbing a bottle of ammonia. He crawled up the bed and settled between Saudia's legs. He sat the bottle down on the bed, grabbed Saudia's pussy lips and clipped both of them off, clitoris included. At this point Saudia was convoluted. Khafre opened the bottle of ammonia and poured it on her wounded vagina. The pain was so intense that Saudia passed out. Khafre left, returned with a bucket of ice water and splashed Saudia in the face. The coldness from the ice water brought Saudia back to semi-consciousness. Khafre wanted her conscious while she suffered. He grabbed an ice pick and jammed it in Saudia's right eye. She wailed in distress but the duct tape suppressed her cries. Khafre then grabbed a hatchet and planted it in the center of Saudia's forehead. Even though the hatchet put a crevice in Saudia's head, she was still alive. In one swift motion, Khafre pulled a Glock 19, snatched the tape and panties from her mouth and jammed it in her throat. Before Saudia could gag, Khafre let off three shots, blowing the back of her brains out. It would be three weeks before Saudia was found by a neighbor.

Chapter Twenty-Five

I Got Something For You

Khafre laid alone in his bed in a state of decadence. He'd avenged the deaths of Shenida and Nilya but didn't know how to feel about it. It had been three weeks since he'd showered. He barely ate anything, and his phone had been ringing constantly. Suicide had been circling his mind perpetually, but the thought of leaving his mother alone kept the barrel out of his mouth. The phone ringing pervaded his thoughts. Instead of ignoring it, he glanced at the phone and saw that it was his mother.

"Yo," mumbled Khafre.

"Hey, baby. How you holding up?" asked Shantel sympathetically. Khafre exhaled before responding.

"Not too good, mama."

"I'm sorry for your loss. Shenida and Nilya was like family to me too so they will be missed. On the contrary though, I'ma need you to pull it together because I need you. I'm pretty sure they wouldn't want'chu to wallow in grief and self-pity. The price we pay for living is death, baby. It's nothing nobody can do to change that. You hear me?"

"I hear you, mama."

"Good! Now get up and get'cha self together. I wanna see you."

"A'ight, mama. I'll be over there."

"Love you, baby."

"Love you too," muttered Khafre. *Click!* Khafre crawled out of bed and made his way to the shower. The hot water galvanized his scalp and every muscle in his body. His dreadlocks hung over his face as he stood under the shower head and contemplated his next move. Thirty-minutes later, Khafre hopped out of the shower and dressed in a YSL sweatsuit and some cocaine-white Forces. He grabbed his pistol and was about to head out but the sight of his bed being messy irked him. He decided to make it before leaving. When Khafre tucked his blanket, he felt his hand slip in a hole that was in the box spring.

"Da fuck?" mumbled Khafre, sliding his mattress to the side. He stuck his hand in the hole and pulled out a bundle of money. Khafre's heart accelerated, adrenaline pumping. He flipped the mattress over. He noticed that there was a sewing pattern around the entire box spring and started ripping it open. When Khafre finished, he was staring at life changing cash with a note atop of it. Puzzled, he reached for the letter and began reading it.

Khafre,
Half of this money is what your father left before gettin' indicted. The other half, I've been saving since he left you in my care. I keep having this dream about me gettin' killed outside of this building, by somebody you know. I have done a lot of grimy shit to a lot of people, Khafre, and I know Karma is makin' her way 'round to me sooner than later. I just wanted to make sure I held my end of the promise I made to your father. I love you so much, and always remember to be forever solid! Never fold! And live your life to the fullest. It's better to be dead than half alive. Your Godmother.
Shenida

An organic sense of comfort seized Khafre as tears fell freely from his eyes, staining the letter. The thought of Shenida securing his future in the midst of fighting her demons was overwhelming. His phone rang again, interrupting his moment of lament. Khafre wiped the tears from his face and answered the phone.

"What's good, ma?"

"Khafre, you still coming?" questioned Shantel.

"Yeah, mama. Give me like an hour."

"An hour?" said Shantel, slightly aggravated.

"I'll be there in an hour, ma. I promise."

"Okay but try to hurry it up. I got something for you."

"Yes, ma'am."

"See you when you get here. I love you."

"Love you too, mama." Khafre hung up and started counting the money. It took him exactly one hour to count all the money. When he was finished, he sat before five hundred thousand. He grabbed a Louis bag from his closet, stuffed three-hundred thousand in it and headed to his mother's house. When Khafre hopped out of his truck, he noticed that Shantel's yard needed a little maintenance. He made a mental note to take care of it. The front door was cracked, so Khafre pushed it open and stepped in.

"Ma!" yelled Khafre with the Louis bag in hand. Moments later, Shantel emerged from the kitchen with her arms outstretched.

"Hey, baby," greeted Shantel, wrapping her arms around Khafre's neck.

"What's up, mama? You okay?"

"Yeah, I'm just in here, frying some chicken. You hungry?" said Shantel with her hands on her hips.

"This for you, mama," Khafre stated, handing Shantel the bag.

"What is it?" asked Shantel, grabbing the bag and placing it on the coffee table. When she unzipped the bag, her mouth gaped open with widened eyes. She then glanced back and forth at Khafre and the money.

"Khafre, where did you get this?" questioned Shantel as her heart rate increased.

"You don't want it?" asked Khafre, reaching for the bag. Shantel snatched the bag closer to her.

"I ain't say all that!"

"Oh, okay," replied Khafre, smiling for the first time since Nilya and Shenida's death.

"How much is it?"

"Three-hunid thousand. And I think you burning yo' chicken up."

"Damit!" yelled Shantel, rushing to the kitchen. Khafre followed behind her.

"It's okay, I ain't burn it," Shantel stated, moving the pan to an eye that wasn't on. She then faced Khafre and smiled.

"What's up, ma?"

"Thank you for the money. I don't know what'chu did to get it, but I need it, so thank you."

"You welcome." Khafre followed his mother's eyes which appeared to be looking at something behind him. He quickly drew his pistol and spun around. Khafre was in such shock that he dropped his gun. Tears began to spill from the wells of his eyes irrepressibly.

"Pops?" asked Khafre in disbelief.

"You ready to put a hole in ya old man on his first day out?" G-Baby asked with a smile on his face. Khafre rushed to his father and buried his head in his chest, wrapping his arms around him. G-Baby held Khafre in return and consoled him as the weight of the world seemed to decrease through the flow of his tears.

"I love you, pops!"

"Love you too." Khafre stepped back and looked into his father's eyes.

"Promise me you won't leave me out here again, pops." Khafre stated with a look of exasperation.

"I'ma keep it real wit'chu, son. I can't promise you that but, as long as I'm here—I got'chu. Now, wipe ya face, man, tighten up. We gotta lot of shit to do today." Khafre wiped his face and turned to his mother.

"Ma! You knew he was here?" questioned Khafre. Shantel nodded with a smile on her face.

"That's why I called you this morning. I told you I had something for you. Y'all go ahead and do y'all thang. I got some shopping to do."

"This shit, crazy!" exclaimed Khafre.

"Boy, watch your mouth," warned Shantel.

"Yes, ma'am."

Chapter Twenty-Six

A Bloody Kiss

It was a bright and sunny afternoon, filled with exuberance. The moment was perfect for Khafre. His father had come home in the midst of his grieving. Khafre didn't pray but he silently thanked the Creator for his father's return. Everybody around Khafre seemed to be dying, and G-Baby took notice of this. For this same reason, he took Khafre to meet his auntie CC and cousins—Hezron and Machi. After that he took him to *Patty's Seafood* to see his grandmother, and step grandfather—D-Dog. He even took him to meet C-Major. Meeting everybody had Khafre a little jaded, so G-Baby took him to the jetty to cool his mind. After thirty-minutes of listening to the ocean in silence, G-Baby told Khafre everything that had happened between him, CC and Mundo. He told Khafre to not hold anything against his auntie CC, because they had made amends. Khafre found the story captivating and was intrigued by the role that everybody played in it. He now knew why killing was second nature to him. He had come from a bloodline of killers.

"So what grandma think about all this?" questioned Khafre.

"She don't know. We kept it between us."

"So who do she think killed Uncle Mundo?"

"The papers said that it was a robbery gone bad. So, that's what she went with." Khafre gazed out into the ocean in deep thought, letting everything he'd just been told settle in. "Come on. I got one more person I want'chu to meet," said G-Baby, standing to leave. On the ride home, Khafre contemplated telling his father about Archie, but was afraid of risking losing him again for killing a cop. He decided that he would kill Archie himself. Fifteen minutes later, G-Baby pulled Khafre's G-wagon in front of the Brown Store.

"Why we here? You wanna see yo' old apartment?" Khafre asked.

"I'll check it out later. I want'chu to meet Wolly."

"The man in the store?" asked Khafre with confusion in his voice.

"Yeah! You met him?"

"I be seeing him around. What'chu want me to meet him for?"

"Because he's a friend of the family and he saved my life.

"How?"

"When I was livin' here a man came from behind the dumpster and attempted to rob me. I end up killing him and Wolly told the police that the man tried to rob him. He took the rap for me. You need a friend like Wolly in the clutch."

"That's some thrill shit! Excuse my language, pops."

"You good. You old enough to stick a nigga in the ground, shid—you old enough to speak freely," G-Baby laughed.

"Just tryin' to respect you, pops."

"Overstood. Now, come on, get out." They got out of the truck and headed inside the store.

"Wolly!" yelled G-Baby.

"Yeah, just a minute," Wolly responded, dropping chicken gizzards in some fresh grease.

"Hurry the fuck up!" said G-Baby.

"Hey! Fuck you, buddy! I told you to—" Wolly stopped mid sentence when he saw that it was G-Baby.

"That's how you treat a paying customer?"

"G-Baby? Ole my goodness! My friend, how are you?"

"I gave that time back—shid, I'm doing wonderful!"

"Somebody tell on you or what, buddy?"

"They gave me a frivolous enhancement for a pistol charge. They had to re-sentence me and gave me time served."

"Well, it's good to see you, my friend. You need anything?"

"Nah. I'm cool. I just wanted you to meet my son, Khafre."

"I didn't know this was your son. I've seen him around. Nice to meet you, Khafre."

"Likewise," replied Khafre.

"If you ever need anything, talk to me, buddy."

"That's what's up. I appreciate that." Khafre smiled.

"He stayin' in the apartment up top," G-Baby informed.

"Oh, yeah? I thought Shenida was living there," Wolly replied.

"She was but she passed."

"I'm sorry to hear that, my friend. I didn't know, buddy."

"It's all good. We gon' talk later. I just wanted my son to meet'chu.

"Okay. Stop by anytime, Khafre." G-Baby and Khafre stepped out of the store.

"He seem like he a'ight," stated Khafre.

"I told you what he did for me."

"Yeah, you did. Check it though, pops. You fresh out, let's go shoppin! Everythang on me."

"I'on really need nothin'. I still got shit I ain't never wear."

"You gained some weight, pops. You need a whole new drobe."

G-Baby examined himself as if he'd just noticed his weight gain.

"Fuck it, let's go. What'chu had in mind?"

"We going to the outlet in Vero. Let me run upstairs real quick."

"Go 'head. I'ma be in the truck," stated G-Baby. Khafre trotted up the stairs that led to his apartment. When he approached his door, he saw that it was ajar.

"Da fuck?" Khafre drew his pistol and entered with caution. He saw that his couch had been cut up and his cabinets were wide open. He entered his bedroom, fearing the worst. Just as he had suspected, his mattress was flipped and all his money was gone. Khafre's heart rate accelerated as he combed his hand through his dreads. As soon as he took a moment to try to wrap his head around who could have done this, he heard rapid gunfire. Khafre got low as if the shots were coming from inside the apartment. When he realized that they were coming from outside, panic enveloped him. He rushed outside and saw that there were no bullet holes in his truck and that his father was still sitting in the truck. Khafre breathed a sigh of relief, until he got closer and noticed the blood on his father's shirt.

"Pops!" screamed Khafre, opening the driver's door. The sight of multiple holes in G-Baby's chest brought tears to Khafre's eyes instantly. He knew that this was his last moments with his father. Even though G-Baby was chasing his breath and coughing up blood, he had the calmest look in his eyes. The expression on his face was not of a man doomed for death. He reached for Khafre and placed a bloody kiss on his forehead.

"I love you, pop!" cried Khafre. G-Baby nodded, assuring Khafre that he knew. Khafre pulled his phone out and attempted to call 911, but G-Baby shook his head by way of saying: *No need to call 911.* He threw his thumb up, letting Khafre know that he was ready to die. Khafre wrapped his arms around his father and held him until his last breath. When Khafre pulled back, he saw that G-Baby's eyes were open. Then he closed his father's eyes. He'd just thanked God for his father's return and now God had taken him away. He felt betrayed as a different type of darkness encompassed his heart and soul.

"Khafre! Come quick!" Khafre looked up and saw Wolly.

"Come before the cops get here," urged Wolly, waving his hand. Khafre followed Wolly in the store. "I'm sorry for what happened to your father. Perhaps this can be of some assistance," declared Wolly as he played the surveillance tape of the parking lot. G-Baby could be seen getting into the driver's seat. Just moments later, he appeared to be talking to someone out of camera view, then—clear as day—a man with dreadlocks stepped in the camera's view with weapon drawn. He pointed the gun inside the window, fired multiple shots then disappeared from the camera's view.

"Archie," whispered Khafre.

Chapter Twenty-Seven

Step Wit'chu

After watching Archie impudently take his father's life, Khafre wanted to comb through the streets and kill every cop in sight. Wolly advised him that reacting off impulse to his father's death could be a mishap. He merely suggested that he lay his father to rest first, then formulate a way to respond. Khafre agreed finally after a heated debate. Khafre knew that a lot of people feared his father, so the only people that would attend his funeral would be his mistresses and family members. He didn't want to risk the safety of his mother and grandmother so he begged his mother to cremate his father. Shantel consulted with Patty, G-Baby's mother and she agreed. A few days after the cremation, Khafre had everybody meet him at the jetty for a candle lighting and the spreading of his father and Shenida's ashes into the ocean. The people that attended the candle lighting were CC, Offtop, Hezron, Machi, Patty, D-dog, Shantel, and C-major. Everybody held a candle and told their most precious, sad, funny, and vicious moment that they've experienced with G-Baby. After spreading the ashes in the ocean, C-major approached Khafre and told him that he was there for him if he ever needed anything. Khafre thanked him for attending and told him that he would call if he needed him. Surprisingly, Hezron and Machi approached Khafre next and asked if they could walk off to the side away from everybody to discuss something of importance. Khafre told his mother that he was stepping off for a minute with his cousins. When they made their way to some massive blocks that sat on the edge of the water, Khafre noticed how tall Machi was and how short and stocky Hezron was. They both had shoulder-length dreadlocks and were dipped in gold from their fingers to their necks.

"Damn, you tall as hell! What'chu 'bout six feet?" asked Khafre.

"Six one," Machi corrected.

"You play ball?"

"I use' to but that ain't me."

"How old you is?"

"Twenty-three," stated Machi."

"What about'chu? You play football?" Khafre asked Hezron.

"Nah! I'm in the streets," Hezron said with pride.

"In the streets, huh? How old you is?"

"Twenty-two."

"Look. I'on mean no disrespect, but what's up?" questioned Machi.

"What'chu mean?" Khafre asked, perplexed.

"G-Baby was our favorite uncle. The reason we wanted to holla at'chu was because if you know who did it, we'll step wit'chu," Machi exclaimed with a look of infallibility in his eyes. Khafre turned to Hezron who had his arms folded across his chest and shaking his head up and down, solidifying Machi's statement.

"Yeah, I know who did it, but I'ma handle it. I can't let y'all put'cha life on the line."

"Man, how old you is?" asked Hezron.

"Sixteen."

Herzon laughed before responding.

"Look man, we been doing this shit. We don't care who it is, we gon' slide," Hezron declared. Khafre couldn't believe what he was hearing.

"I'ma keep it real, wit'chu. I thought y'all was just two spoiled rotten ass niggaz," Khafre admitted.

"Our father do spoil us but don't get it twisted. We smokin' shit," Hezron confirmed with conviction.

"Y'all know Archie?"

"Yeah, he be fuckin' wit' my pops, harassing him and shit. What about him?" asked Hezron.

"He killed my father. He thought my father had something to do wit' his partner gettin', killed."

"It ain't nothin' else to talk about. When we ride?" asked Machi.

***

Two nights later, the trio manoeuvred through the city meticulously in a black-on-black van in search of their target, but Archie was nowhere to be found. Khafre had an arsenal in the back of the van given to him by Wolly. The price for the weapons was Wolly's wishes of death upon the perpetrator that killed G-Baby. Khafre told Wolly to consider his wish granted.

"Man, we been ridin' around for hours, lookin' for this nigga," enunciated Hezron seethingly.

"Patience, lil' bra. Somebody dying tonight! It ain't gotta be Archie. We can catch him another time. Anyone of his lil' partners can get it. That mean anybody wit' a badge!" stated Hezron.

"That's what the fuck I'm talkin' 'bout!" replied Khafre from behind the wheel.

"Say no more," said Machi. Khafre was driving down 39th when he spotted a sheriff parked to his left on Sloan Avenue. "We got action," asserted Khafre, making a right on Sloan Street. Two houses down on the right sat an empty house. Khafre pulled in front of it, cut his lights and parked.

"Let me hit 'em," begged Hezron.

"Nah, you get the next one. I got it," said Machi, grabbing a .30 from the arsenal. It was already a hole in the back window of the van the size of a hockey puck. Machi placed the top of the rifle through the hole and peered through the digital scope that calculated the distance between him and his target. The distance read 35 yards. Machi noticed that the officer appeared to be looking at something on his laptop. Machi aligned the cross hairs in between the officer's eyes, exhaled then pulled the trigger. Through the scope, Machi witnessed the .30-06 Springfield rounds blow out the top of the officer's head.

"You hit 'em?" asked Hezron excitedly.

"Yeah, let's roll out," replied Machi. Khafre pulled off sleekly and turned his lights on once they were further up the street.

"How you know if he dead or not?" questioned Hezron.

"Kuz I seen the top of his head explode. That shit was wild," Machi asserted nonchalantly.

"Okay. It's my turn. Go down 17th and pull behind that old, Mexican club.

"What's over there?" asked Machi.

"You'll see." A couple minutes later, Khafre was approaching 17th and Okeechobee. Before making a right turn into the Mexican club that was closed, Khafre noticed a police cruiser backed in to his left at the circle K.

"See I know his ass was gon' be there eating and shit," Hezron stated, tucking his dreadlocks in a beanie hat atop his head. Khafre rounded the building that was dark and parked under a colossal oak tree that shadowed everything beneath it. Hezron slid his gloves on and grabbed a Glock 19. "Keep the van running, I'll be back in a jiffy," Hezron declared, hopping out of the van with his hands in his black hoodie. Instead of going in front of the store where the cameras were, Hezron posted on the side of the store. Moments later, a white couple walked up heading toward the store.

"Excuse me! Can one of you guys be so kind enough to spare a little change," Hezron asked in the most proper grammar he could muster.

"Dude, get a job," replied the white male.

"Thanks anyway," said Hezron. The couple b-lined straight for the officer's cruiser and told him that there was a black guy begging on the side of the store. The officer wasted no time getting out of his car to approach Hezron. He flashed the light in Hezron's face with his hand on his gun.

"Hey, buddy, you can't be up here begging folks for their hard-earned money. Get a job! I'm gonna have to ask you to leave, pal."

"Okay, officer, no problem," assured Hezron. A couple of high school girls laughing before entering the store diverted the officer's attention away from Hezron.

Boc! Boc! Boc! Hezron squeezed three shots through his hoodie, hitting the officer in his midsection, dropping him. Hezron then snatched the Glock from his hoodie, stood over the cop and gave him the rest of the clip with no clemency. He sprinted back to the truck and hopped in. They made a clean getaway. As they headed to the other side of town, Khafre let it be known that he was impressed. He was elated to know that he had folks that were just as nefarious as him. He felt as if their demons had a connection and he vowed to congeal a solid relationship with his cousins.

"I'm sayin' though—y'all peeped how I stood over that boy? I'ma dog wit' it!" Hezron stated, laughing.

"You did that," Khafre admitted.

"I ain't impressed," lied Machi.

"Nigga, my gun game nice! Stop playin' wit' me," said Hezron. Khafre drove past Miranda's subs on 39th and spotted another patrol car with an officer sitting in it. On the side of Miranda's was a two-story house that was abandoned, with a brown gate between the two. Khafre backed in the desolate property and parked.

"Machi, hand me that pineapple grenade from back there," instructed Khafre.

"Grenade? You on some other shit," exclaimed Hezron. Machi found the grenade and handed it to Khafre.

"Machi, get in the driver seat," demanded Khafre, hopping out of the van. He then made his way out of the yard, and around the gate and proceeded to Miranda's. Khafre knew that there were no cameras in Miranda's so he went in and purchased two macarons. He then walked outside and ate both of the macarons a few feet away from the police cruiser. Khafre noticed the officer rolled down his windows.

"What'chu got there? Macarons?" asked the officer.

"Yes, sir. I'm thinking about buying a few more," Khafre replied, trying to sound and appear as less threatening as possible.

"Those little fuckers sure are tasty, aren't they?" asked the officer, being friendly.

"Yes, sir,"

"Here, I gotta dozen of 'em. Have one," offered the officer. Khafre approached the car and grabbed a macaron from the box. He quickly devoured it.

"Thank you, officer."

"No problem, brother," replied the white officer.

"Do you think you could direct me to the turnpike?" asked Khafre.

'Sure. When you leave out of her—"

"Can you write it down for me please?"

"Sure, brother, hold on," stated the officer, placing the box on the passenger seat. While doing so, the officer felt something drop in his lap. He looked to see what it was but it rolled off of his lap and under the seat. When he looked to see where Khafre had gone, all he caught was a glimpse of his shoe going over the gate. By the time Khafre reached the van, the police cruiser exploded. Hezron and Machi flinched and got low.

"Come on, let's go! Hurry up!" yelled Khafre. Machi got on the gas, and they slithered away unnoticed.

Chapter Twenty-Eight

Paradigm

A week later, Shantel picked Khafre up from Shenida's old house. Archie knowing where he laid his head didn't sit well with Khafre. He'd decided to stay at Shenida's until he found and killed Archie. Before G-Baby's death, he'd introduced Khafre to Baby Haitian in case of emergencies. Shantel was now headed to the carwash on 29th street so Khafre could pick up his G-wagon from Baby Haitian.

"Khafre, why you won't just get rid of that truck? I'll trade it in and get'chu somethin' nicer," Shantel said.

"My father gifted me that truck for my sixteenth birthday. The valve of that is paramount! I'll never get rid of my truck, mama."

"Well, I didn't know he bought it for you. I won't bring it up again," Shantel assured.

"I appreciate if you didn't," Khafre replied, gazing out of the window.

"Okay. I forgot to tell you—when your father got outta the Feds, he came home with a hunid and fifty thousand dollars. I'on know what he was doing in there but it's yours, if you want it."

"Just keep it for me until I need it, mama."

"That's fine. How you like yo' cousins—Hezron and Machi?"

"They cool. I'm finna go chill wit' 'em after I pick my truck up."

"That's good. Listen to me though. I want'chu to be careful riding around wit' them guns. Three police officers got killed like a week ago and one of them was by a grenade. How the hell somebody get their hands on a grenade?"

"It's possible, ma."

"Well, that shit got the Feds crawling through our lil' city, so be careful," Shantel advised, pulling into the carwash.

"I heard about that. I'ma be careful, mama," Khafre stated, kissing his mother on the cheek before departing.

"Love you!" Shantel rolled down her window and yelled.

"Love you too," Khafre yelled over his shoulder then headed towards Baby Haitian.

"What's good, lil' goon?" greeted Baby Haitian, dapping Khafre up.

"Just coolin'! Shid, what I owe you?"

"This one on me, lil' goon. Me and yo' daddy did a lot of bidness, ya heard."

"Respect!"

"All the time. You know yo' father was treacherous but he was a solid nigga. When it came to standin' on that bidness, he was the paradigm. Wit' with that being said, it was an honor to clean yo' father's blood. And I say that wit' the utmost respect, lil' goon."

"I'm feelin' that," exclaimed Khafre, looking Baby Haitian in his eyes.

"Anytime you need a clean-up, call me. I'm here for you, lil' goon," Baby Haitian stated, handing Khafre his keys.

"It's most definitely gon' be some work in the near future for you." Baby Haitian smiled and dapped Khafre up before walking off. Moments later, Khafre's phone rung.

"Yeah?" answered Khafre, getting in his truck.

"What up, kuz?" asked Hezron.

"Shid, I was headed y'all way now."

"Okay, that's what's up! Make sure you bring them branches. We tryna step again," asserted Hezron excitedly.

"Say none, I'm in the air now. Tell Machi I said what's up."

"Already."

Khafre headed to Shenida's house to go strap up before meeting up with his cousins. Instead of pulling in the backyard, he backed his truck in the front yard and popped the trunk. Khafre then ran into the house and grabbed two lightweight SIGM 400s that he'd gotten from Wolly and loaded them in the trunk. When Khafre pulled out, he noticed a Scion that was parked a few houses back pull behind him, keeping its distance. Khafre came to Avenue H and 27th Street then made a left. Looking in his rearview, he saw that the Scion made a left too. His heart began to race, not knowing if it was them boys or the Smackers. He quickly made a right on 27th and Avenue I, then made a left into a corner store on 25th and Avenue I. Khafre leaped in the back seat and grabbed one of the SIG M 400s but the Scion kept going, making a right on 25th street. Khafre breathed a sigh of relief.

Damn, this shit crazy, thought Khafre. He needed something to calm his nerves, so he got out and headed into the store. As soon as Khafre walked in, he saw a high school friend sitting at a slot machine that the Arabian owner put in to dig deeper into poor people's pockets. He walked past her and grabbed a *Red Stripe* from the cooler. When he turned around, Toya was standing there with her hands on her hips.

"Damn, stranger! Yo' don't know nobody now, huh? Ya lil' name rangin in the streets. You brand new now, huh?" said Toya.

"Nah. I saw you was on the machine and shit. I ain't wanna be rude and shit."

"I guess. Give me a hug." Toya stretched her arms out and Khafre gave her a half hug. "When the summer over, you coming back to school, right?"

"Yeah, I might."

"Ya might?"

"Yeah. Look, I gotta slide. I'ma see you around, Toya," Khafre stated, heading to the counter to pay for his beer.

"Three-dollars!" said the Arab, not even asking for an ID. Khafre paid and stepped out of the store.

"Don't move, lil' bitch ass nigga!" Khafre stopped in his tracks and attempted to turn around to see the perpetrator. "Move again! I'ma blow yo' fuckin' head clean off yo' shoulders!" Khafre recognized the voice and didn't move. He knew the gunman was a killer.

"Bring 'em in!" As soon as Khafre heard those words, unmarked cars pulled up from every direction. Four men in masks hopped out of a Durango and grabbed Khafre. The others went straight to the trunk of Khafre's truck and grabbed the weapons. While the task force were putting Khafre in the truck, he saw that the gunman was Archie. It was then that he realized that Archie was in the Scion and had watched him load the weapons in the truck.

***

Khafre had been sitting in an interrogation room for two hours with his hands cuffed behind his back before anyone came to question him. He was cold, hungry, and tired. Finally, Archie made his way in the room, bearing a smile that told Khafre he was fucked. Once Archie sat across from Khafre, he gave one of his cronies behind the glass a look that said: *cut the surveillance tape.*

"What dey do lil' nigga?" questioned Archie, still smiling. Khafre looked his father's killer in the eyes and smirked before replying.

"I thought you was gon' keep it in the streets, officer," Khafre stated sardonically.

"Oh, I plan to. I just wanted to take you out'cha element for a while. Ain't no guns in prison, lil' nigga and you headed straight to gladiator camp. And when you come home, *if* you make it home, I'ma be right there to put yo' lil' bitch ass in a box next to yo' father." Khafre's jaw tensed as Archie laughed before continuing.

"As much as I hate your father, I respect how he died like a man. He didn't panic or beg for his life. He took that whole clip with honor." Khafre looked Archie in his eyes, then spat in his face.

Archie wiped his face with the sleeve of his shirt.

"That one is on me. But this vacation to Paris I'm finna take is all on you. Racks on racks, lil' nigga," laughed Archie.

"You a real bitch ass nigga!" declared Khafre. "You go ahead and enjoy yo' lil vacation. Whereever them crackaz send me, nigga, I'm forever solid! When I touch down, you know what it is," Khafre stated cockily.

"Yeah, whatever, lil' nigga," replied Archie, waving his hand dismissively. "I tell you what. You ain't gotta wait until you get outta prison to avenge yo' father. Tell me where you got them guns from and I'll let'chu go tonight."

"Shid, I'll tell you whatever you wanna know. All you gotta do is blow my dick first, bitch ass nigga! Get the fuck out my face, clown ass nigga!"

Archie laughed.

"You know yo' mama gotta fat ass. I see why yo' father peed in that pussy. I'ma take real good care of all that ass while you gone," exclaimed Archie, getting up to leave. A few moments after Archie left, Khafre's mother walked in with teary eyes and hugged Khafre's neck.

"Baby, you okay? They are not suppose' to question you without me present. Did they?"

"Nah, mama, everythang cool," lied Khafre.

"They told me you got caught with military guns. I told you not to ride around like that," cried Shantel. "Don't worry I'ma get'chu a lawyer."

"Don't do that. Save yo' money, ma," Khafre insisted.

"Boy, we got plenty money. I'm getting a lawyer."

"I'm tired, mama. I need a break. Just let me go lay down for a while. When I come home, I'll have my head right." Shantel shook her head in disbelief.

"I guess if that's what'chu want. I love you, boy."
"Love you, too, mama."

Khufu

Chapter Twenty-Nine

You're Sweet

During Khafre's first week in jail, he slept like a bear. The weight of the world had him so exhausted that he didn't even shower or eat, which was a plus for his cellmate. He ate everything that Khafre didn't touch. Two months after being incarcerated, Khafre finally started to get with the flow of how things operate behind bars. His cellmate was a cool and hyperactive dude named Nate, who had been in and out of the system since he was twelve. He schooled Khafre on jail and prison edict, to prepare him for the hell that awaited him at gladiator prison. He even taught Khafre how to be "swift", a prison term for being calm and smooth while defeating your opponent in hand-to-hand combat. He taught Khafre everything he knew but nothing could prepare Khafre for the unknown. He would have to learn through trial and error.

Eight months later, Khafre was adjudicated as an adult and sentenced to five years in prison. The bus ride to Orlando Reception Center was nerve-racking. Khafre was a killer at heart, but he knew that he was headed to a world which he'd never been. When the bus pulled into the prison, Khafre wondered why everybody had their heads in their laps. He'd missed the pep talk that the guards gave before leaving the county jail. Moments later, a guard opened the back door and came aboard. When he got to Khafre, he slapped him in the back of his head.

"What the fuck makes you so special boy? Don't'chu see everybody sucking their own dick? Get that head in you lap, boy!"

"Sir, yes, sir!" yelled Khafre, putting his head in his lap.

"Get the fuck off my bus!" All inmates rushed to get off the bus in shackles, tripping over each other in the process. Khafre was the last one off the bus, prompting the guard to slap him in the back of the head again. All inmates were instructed to line up along the fence so their shackles could be removed.

"Turn around and strip!" After stripping, an orderly swept through and picked up everybody's county jail uniforms. The guard stepped in front of Khafre.

"Get your hands off that pecker, boy!"

'Sir, yes, sir!" yelled Khafre, exposing his manhood to the guard. "Open yo' mouth, lift your tongue, lift you top lip, pull your bottom lip down, rub your hands through your head, turn around, lift your feet left, right, squat and cough!" Another orderly swept through and handed each inmate a pair of boxers. "Inside, now!" All inmates rushed in the reception center. The next three hours of orientation drained and aggravated Khafre, especially when he had to sit in the chair and watch his shoulder-length dreadlocks drop from his head. Before anybody could be released from orientation to their dorm, they had to memorize and recite their extended day creed. By the time it was Khafre's turn, he'd already had the creed memorized.

"This is my extended day creed, sir! Watch your thoughts, they become your words / Watch your words, they become your actions / Watch your actions, they become your habits / Watch your habits, they become your lifestyle / Watch your lifestyle, it becomes your destiny / This is my extended day creed, sir!" recited Khafre.

"Move along," said the guard. Khafre grabbed his blanket and headed to his dorm. He didn't recognize anybody from his hometown, so he kept it pushing to his room, and noticed that he didn't have a roommate. Khafre began making up his bed, when he heard his dorm being called for commissary. He half made his bed and rushed out to commissary. When he got back, he put his food up and decided to call his mother. Shantel picked up on the third ring.

"Hello?"

"Yeah, what's up, ma?"

"Hey, baby. I miss you and love you so much."

"Love you too, mama."

"How is it? You see anybody you know?"

"I'm at the reception center ma. It ain't too much to be worried about here. It's the main camp that's gon' be a problem. And I didn't see nobody from the city."

"Well, just stay to yourself. Don't let nobody take nothing from you and don't let nobody put their hands on you. You hear me?" asked Shantel.

"Ain't nobody gon' take nothin', from me or put their hands on me. The officers the only ones who been putting their hands on me." Khafre got angry all over again, thinking about the officer who slapped him in the head.

"Listen. I know you in them white folks' world right now and you gotta take a lot of their shit. Now, I don't want'chu to get no extra time added to your sentence, but if you ever feel like you've been disrespected to a degree where your manhood is being tested, do what'chu gotta do. I support whatever decision you make."

"Thank you, mama. I needed to hear that."

"I sent you enough money to last you until you come home."

"I saw that."

"Oh, yeah, your cousins—Hezron and Machi—called to check on you. I told them you was okay." A smile graced Khafre's face as he thought about his cousins.

"Next time they call, tell 'em I said what's up. Mama, I gotta go. I'm tired from orientation."

"Okay, I'll tell 'em. Love you, baby."

"Love you too, mama." Khafre hung up the phone. As soon as he entered his room, he noticed that his locker was open and all his food was gone. This inflamed Khafre profoundly. He walked out of his room and addressed the whole dorm.

"Which one of you poe ass niggaz stole my shit?" yelled Khafre, causing the dorm to go silent.

"I did, nigga!" yelled a light-skinned kid named Mane. Mane was eighteen, two years older than Khafre, standing 5'11. He was a permanent at the reception center and loved to test all the new cocks that came in. Khafre wasted no time approaching Mane who had slid out of view of the officer station. When Khafre got within arm's reach, Mane threw a hard left, but Khafre slipped it and countered with a two-piece, dropping Mane perilously. Khafre backed up, giving Mane time to recover.

"I'on want it like that. Get up, nigga! Tighten up!" taunted Khafre. Mane got up, still dazed, and threw a straight left and a right. Instead of countering, Khafre bobbed and weaved both punches, and pulled Mane's pants down. The moment Mane dropped his guard to pull his pants back up Khafre slapped him, drawing chatter and laughter from the crowd.

"I'on even wanna fight'chu no more, nigga, yo' sweet! Go get my shit before I punish you for real!" declared Khafre.

"I ain't givin' you—" before Mane could finish his statement, Khafre peppered him with a three-punch combination, dropping him again. Khafre kicked Mane in the face and ordered him to go get his commissary. Not waiting around to see if Mane would bring his food, Khafre went to go take a shower. When he came back, all his food plus more was laid out across his bed. As time went on, Mane explained to Khafre that he was just testing his heart. Eventually, they formed a bond until Khafre was shipped to his main camp.

Chapter Thirty

The River

When Khafre got off the bus at Indian River, he had to go through the same process as far as stripping, squatting, and coughing. Once he was dressed, an attractive young black guard gave him and other inmates a speech as to how things ran at the River. When she was finished with her speech, she addressed Khafre.

"What the fuck is you lookin' at?" asked the guard.

"Who? Me?" asked Khafre, confused.

"Yeah, you! Who the fuck you lookin' at?"

"You doing all the talkin', so I'm lookin' at'chu," exclaimed Khafre.

"Oh, you think yo' tough, huh?" asked the female guard, squinting.

"I'on want no smoke wit'chu. You got that."

"I know I do. We gon' see, 'bout all this tough shit," said the guard.

Orderlies began bringing the inmates their mattresses. After everybody was giving one, they were told to head to the laundry room. Khafre was the last one to enter the laundry room. As soon as he crossed the threshold, he was hit from both sides and dropped.

"You gon' break it off!" yelled both inmates, referring to Khafre's commissary. They pummeled Khafre with kicks and punches as he tried desperately to remove the mattress that he was carrying off of him.

"Fuck you, nigga! I ain't breaking shit off!" stated Khafre. While the two inmates were doing a number on Khafre, he heard a female behind him laughing. When the inmates finished with Khafre, one of his eyes were closed and both of his lips were busted up. Khafre got up a bit dazed and saw that the female voice he heard was the same one that he'd had words with.

"Yeah, tough ass nigga," the guard mocked him. Khafre looked at her with murder in his eyes, nodded, grabbed his mattress and picked his laundry up from the window. Khafre was assigned to K-

Block, which was the worst block on the pound. As soon as Khafre entered the block, inmates were gawking and ready to pounce. He even saw inmates banging on the glass, doing sign language telling other inmates to crush him. *Damn, this shit crazy*, thought Khafre. When Khafre reached his assigned room, he noticed that the only window in the room was a small one on the door. He entered and put his mattress on the top bunk. Before he could get a chance to make his bed, two inmates made their way in.

"What up, bra? Where you from? What'chu bang?" asked the smaller one of the two who attempted to help Khafre make his bed. Khafre took a step back, peeping their body language.

"Killa Kounty, nigga!" Khafre yelled before dropping the smaller inmate with a right. When the bigger inmate attempted to sucker punch Khafre, he slipped it and wrapped up with him. Khafre put his right leg behind the inmate's left leg and tripped him to the ground. Before Khafre could go to work on him, three more inmates rushed in and cracked Khafre in the back of his head with a lock and sock. Khafre winced and fell over, trying severely to cover himself.

"You gon' break it off!" yelled two of the inmates.

"Fuck you, niggaz! You gotta kill me!" replied Khafre.

"Chow time! Chow time!" informed the guard.

"Before it's all over, you gon' break it off, nigga," one of the inmates stated with confidence before all five inmates departed for chow. Khafre now had two knots on his head, two busted lips, and both of his eyes were nearly closed. Chow was mandatory, so Khafre got himself together and headed to the cafeteria. On his way out of the dorm, Khafre passed a guard.

"Damn, boy! You better learn how to duck or something," the guard said mockingly, laughing in Khafre's face. Khafre just kept it pushing. Once outside, all inmates were in formation for cadence call. When Khafre fell in line, he noticed that the inmate who was leading cadence was the same inmate who hit him with a lock. Khafre made a mental note to crush him once the opportunity presented itself.

"Base check, base check! Squad attention!
K-dorm! Your forward March! Yo' left, yo' left, right, yo' left!
Up in the morning, 'round 4:30 (hard work, work)
Teacher trying to educate me (hard work, work)
I got'cha sister legs (high)
I got the chevy sittin' (high)
Yo' left, yo' left, right, yo' left!"

They marched all the way to the chow hall, and once they were seated, they only had three minutes to eat. It was difficult for Khafre to eat with a busted mouth and—on top of that—he could barely see. By the time he'd ate only the drumstick from his chicken, the guard was yelling: *Time up.* All inmates rushed to put their trays up and headed outside where they marched back to their dorm. It had been a rough day for Khafre; so, after chow, he was ready to lie down and get some rest. When he got to his room, it was two inmates in there that he hadn't seen earlier.

"Aye, slide jit! Yo' know what time it is," declared one of the inmates. Khafre attempted to rush him but was attacked from behind. Ten inmates stormed the room and took turns kicking and punching Khafre.

"You gon' break it off?" a few inmates asked in unison.

"Fuck no! You gotta kill me, bitch ass niggaz!" yelled Khafre.

Two inmates picked up a locker and told the others to move out of the way. When Khafre looked up, he saw the locker coming down and put his hands up in an attempt to block it, but the force from it still smashed his head into the concrete. Khafre was dazed but not completely out of it.

"You gon' break it off?" asked another inmate.

"Kill me, nigga!" yelled Khafre. A guard walked by and peeped in the cell.

"Hey, y'all hold it down in there, now!" advised the guard.

"C.O.—C.O!" yelled Khafre. A few inmates laughed.

"He ain't gon' help you, nigga! You gon' break it off?"

"Fuck no, nigga! Kill me!" They stomped Khafre a few more minutes then left him lying on the floor with his face unrecognizable. Khafre noticed that one of the inmates didn't leave the room. Moments later, it dawned on him that it was his cellmate. He was in too much pain to get revenge on his cellie but made a mental note to take care of him later.

"Bra, they gon' punish you everyday until you break it off. Just break it off, bra. You can't beat fifteen niggaz," said Khafre's cellie whose name was Boobie.

"Da fuck I look like, nigga? I'ma real killer," replied Khafre with conniption. Boobie just laid back and shook his head at Khafre's stubbornness.

***

The next morning at 3:30 a.m., while Khafre lay in his rack sleeping, Boobie opened the door to their cell and let five inmates in. They rushed in and commenced to beat Khafre with locks in socks. The first blow to the head caused Khafre to grab his head then stand to his feet. Still half sleep, it took a moment for him to realize what was going on. He traversed back and forth on his rack while the five inmates swung their locks at his feet and kneecaps.

"You gon' break it off?" question one of the inmates.

"You got my mama fucked up, nigga!" yelled Khafre then leaped off the top bunk, drop-kicking one of the inmates in the face, knocking him down. It was a bold attempt for Khafre which proved to be fatal. The other four inmates added more knots to Khafre's head. When the locks started hitting Khafre in the same spot, the knots began to split open and leak blood. Finally, the beating stopped. Two inmates held Khafre's arms while two held his legs. The fifth one pulled Khafre's pants down and pulled out a bic lighter. Seeing this, Khafre snatched his arms away from their grip and covered his dick and balls. The two inmates were punching Khafre in his face as he turned his head left to right and twisted his body to keep the other inmate from burning his balls.

"Ya gon' break it off?" questioned the inmate with the lighter.

"Fuck you, nigga! Gotta kill me, nigga!" stated Khafre, blowing air whenever he could in an attempt to blow the flame out. The inmate with the lighter couldn't get to Khafre's balls but managed to burn Khafre's ass cheeks.

"Man, this nigga crazy! He ain't gon' break it off," said the inmate with the lighter.

"Oh, he gon' break it off, eventually," replied one of the other inmates.

"Y'all come on," instructed the inmate who had the lighter. Later on that day, Khafre decided to call his mother. When she accepted the call, Khafre could hear the excitement in her voice.

"Hey, baby. How you doing?" asked Shantel, oblivious to the trauma Khafre was being subjected to.

"Look, ma! I'm callin' to let'chu know I might not make it home."

"What'chu mean?" questioned Shantel, panicking.

"I love you." *Click!* Khafre hung up on his mother. He could barely see but was able to spot the inmate who had burned his ass cheeks, sitting in the dayroom. Khafre approached him from behind and hit him with a right hook on the right side of his chin, rattling his brain. The inmate, whose name was Smokey, looked up and fell face first. Khafre flipped him over and put his thumbs in Smokey's eyes, trying to remove them from their sockets but a guard who had just entered the dorm sprayed Khafre and cuffed him. The first week in the hole, Khafre was without a cellmate. His wounds had healed a little and his eyes were now opened, enabling him to see. He had time to think and meditate on how he was gon' survive in the hell that he was in. He came to the conclusion that he would no longer be punished. He would be the one inflicting punishment. One night, a little after 8:30 p.m. the flap to his cell opened.

"Moss, cuff up!' ordered the guard. Cuffed up, Khafre got up and put his back to the door. The cell then popped open and another inmate was brought in who was also cuffed up. Once the door was secured, Khafre put his back to the door to let the guard uncuff him. When the cuffs were off, Khafre laid back in his rack. The other inmate's cuffs were also removed.

"What's good, my nigga? They call me Duke." Khafre ignored Duke and continued to gaze at the bunk above him. Seeing that Khafre wasn't friendly, Duke climb in the top bunk and laid down until it was chow time. When the flap opened, Khafre grabbed his tray and sat it on the small desk that was in the room. Duke grabbed his tray, turned around and saw Khafre standing there. Before he could finish recognizing the demons in Khafre's eyes, Khafre had hit him square on his chin and grabbed his tray before he dropped. It was the first time Khafre ever saw someone snore after being knocked out. After eating both of their trays, Khafre climbed back in his rack and went to sleep. Khafre took all of Duke's trays for the next twenty days that he had in the hole.

Chapter Thirty-One

Fast Eddie

Before Khafre knew it, two and a half years had passed him by. He had built a reputation for being the swiftest inmate on the pound. Nobody wanted to fight Khafre because it was nearly impossible to even touch him. The same pain that was inflicted upon Khafre, he was now inflicting upon others. There was another inmate named Fast Eddie, who was swift, but not as swift as Khafre. He envied and despised the respect that inmates gave Khafre, and he wanted to challenge him to put an end to what he thought was a facade. Khafre was in his room, making one of his do-boys make his bed, when Eddie and three more inmates calmly walked in his room.

"Get out and come back in ten minutes. This won't take long," Khafre told his do-boy. Ryan, which was the name of Khafre's do-boy, did as he was told.

"What's up, nigga?" Khafre asked aggressively.

"You know what it is, nigga, slide!" replied Eddie.

"All y'all tryna line that shit up? Or you wanna get embarrassed by yo'self?"

"I'on need no help for you bitch ass nigga," declared Eddie, putting his set up. Khafre stood in parade rest with his hands behind his back. Eddie threw a quick two piece, but Khafre weaved both punches, then spinned on his left pivot. Eddie didn't even realize that Khafre was on the side of him. Khafre kissed Eddie on his cheek then pushed him.

"Eddie, you sweet! Go 'bout'cha bidness now!" warned Khafre.

"Come on, fuck nigga!" yelled Eddie, as he rushed Khafre with another two piece. Khafre again weaved both punches, grabbed Eddie's back arm, spun him around and pulled his pants down. Eddie pulled his pants back up and turned back around.

"Come on, man, I thought you was *Fast Eddie*. Get out my room. I'on wanna fight'chu no more, man."

"You got that. I can't do nothing wit'chu," admitted Eddie, holding his fist out to dapp Khafre up. Khafre reached out to dapp Eddie up, but Eddie attempted to sucker punch Khafre. It proved futile. Khafre sidestepped Eddie and broke his jaw, dropping him. While Khafre started stomping Eddie, the other three inmates rushed him. Khafre's block game was nice, so the damage was minuscule. All of a sudden, two of the inmates dropped to the floor. Khafre threw a short right hook, dropping the last inmate. When Khafre looked up, he was staring at Chico Sito. Sito was the same Puerto Rican who helped Khafre kidnap Saudia's mother.

"Sito?" asked Khafre.

"What's up, nigga?" replied Sito, smiling. "Y'all niggaz get the fuck out!" demanded Sito. Knowing who Sito was, they did as they were told. This was Sito's second bid. He was the swiftest inmate during his first bid and everybody knew it. Inmates told tales about Sito as if he were some kind of urban legend.

"How long you been here?" asked Khafre.

"I just got here. I'm back on violation."

"I been hearing bout'cha, boy," said Sito.

"I heard bout'chu too, nigga," said Khafre. "How you violated?" asked Khafre.

"Smokin' a lil' reefer. Why they got'chu?"

"You remember that bitch ass police you pulled yo' gun on?"

"Yeah!"

"He was watchin' me and shit. The nigga saw me loading two choppaz in my truck and put the law on me."

"Damn! What they gave you?"

"Five, but shid, I been down two and a half."

"Yeah, that ain' t nothin'! You can do the rest of that on the toilet," Sito said jokingly.

"You need something?" asked Khafre.

"Nah. I'on want nothin' from you. I'ma go take one of them niggaz shit who just left outta here."

"Shid, I'm wit'cha," stated Khafre.

"Leggo!" For the next six months, Khafre and Sito terrorized everything in their path. Khafre was turning nineteen and he had gotten word that he was going to be transferred. Khafre hadn't forgotten about his cellie opening the door to let five inmates run in on him. He told Sito to watch his back while he bought Boobie a move. Sito told Khafre that he would see him on the outs, and dapped him up. Khafre moved proficiently through the dayroom where Boobie was watching TV. In one swift motion, Khafre wrapped his arm around Boobie's neck and began stabbing him in the top of his head repeatedly. When Khafre turned Boobie loose, he fell and lay on the tiled floor, bleeding. Khafre walked off and headed to his room. After authorities rolled the camera back, they came and grabbed Khafre. The guards were telling Khafre that he was going to be charged with second-degree murder, because Boobie was pronounced dead on the scene. What the guards failed to tell Khafre was that Boobie was revived on the helicopter on the way to the hospital. All that night, Khafre was thinking of how he would never see the light of day again. Early that morning, a guard who was feeding told Khafre that Boobie hadn't died. Khafre breathed a sigh of relief and thanked the guard. After sitting in the hole for nine months, Khafre was shipped and placed on C.M. for the remainder of his bid. When he was released, his cousins were there to welcome him back in the world in style. Offtop had rented a stretch Bentley, and sent word for Khafre to come see him once he was released.

"What up, family?' asked Machi, dapping and hugging Khafre's neck.

"What's up wit' it?" answered Khafre, smiling.

"Damn, you done got'cha weight up!" stated Hezron, dapping Khafre up and pulling him in close. "You ready to handle bidness," said Hezron.

"Already!"

"That's what I love to hear," exclaimed Hezron, opening the door for Khafre. When Khafre slid in the limo, he noticed two young ladies holding bottles of Remy.

"Welcome home, Khafre," greeted the two snow bunnies in unison.

"What's good, ladies?" replied Khafre, grabbing one of the bottles.

Both women made an attempt to seduce Khafre.

"Ladies, ladies!" Khafre stated briskly. No disrespect to the two of you beautiful creatures, but I'm cool. Leave me ya numbers and I promise you I'ma get wit'chu later."

"Awww!" pouted both Hanna and Samantha. "You promise to call?" asked Hanna.

"That's my word," assured Khafre.

"Okay, sexy," flirted Samantha.

"Nigga! You just did five years! You don't want no pussy?" Hezron asked with a quizzical expression.

"Pussy, gon' be there. I got bidness to handle," said Khafre.

"Oh, okay, shid! Say no more. Aye, driver, drop these hoez off!" instructed Hezron. After dropping Hanna and Samantha off, Machi handed Khafre the new Galaxy 12 and a "bazooka green" Davidson's special edition Glock 19 holding fifteen hollow tips.

"Good lookin', my nigga," Khafre asserted appreciatively.

"I already set'chu up a Facebook," mentioned Machi. All kind of people been hittin' you up.

"Oh yeah? Shid! We going live in a minute then," said Khafre.

"Swing me by the graveyard," Hezron said to the driver. Ten minutes later they were pulling up to the graveyard, located on 13th Street. "Y'all niggaz strapped?" questioned Khafre.

"No need for the rhetorical questions," Machi replied with a devilish grin.

"Let's roll," said Khafre, grabbing one of the bottles of Remy. "One of y'all niggaz got somethin' to roll up?"

"You—know—it!" said Hezron, pulling a grovel leaf from his pocket and proceeded to roll up two blunts of purple sour diesel. They all walked past the graves that didn't have tombstones. The families of those buried without tombstones could not afford any. Then they headed towards the ones that had tombstones. When Khafre reached Nilya's grave, he squatted and kissed her tombstone.

"What up wit' it, big head?" said Khafre, taking a sip from the Remy bottle. "It's been hard without'chu, girl. I miss and I love you forever!"

"Here, fam," said Hezron, passing Khafre the blunt. Khafre took a toke from the blunt then continued his conversation with Nilya.

"I been speakin' to the wind for assistance, and I swear it's like I can hear you in my head, guiding me out here." Khafre hit the blunt again then passed it back to Hezron. He chased the smoke with a swallow of Remy.

"I want'chu to know that I tortured that hoe Saudia. You made me promise you and I kept my word. I killed her mama too." Hearing that made Hezron's eyes widen with excitement. Machi remained reserved as if he already knew. "I'ma kill any and everything related or affiliated with Kurt and Saudia," declared Khafre, taking another sip from the Remy bottle. "Oh yeah," added Khafre, laughing before he continued. "I killed yo' lil' boy friend too. I shoulda wiped his rose a long time ago," proclaimed Khafre, shaking his head. "I love you, girl! Talk to you later." Khafre stood up and motioned for his cousins to follow him.

"You a'ight?" asked Machi concernedly.

"Never better," affirmed Khafre. Two minutes later, Khafre stopped in front of Kurt's grave and handed Machi his phone.

"What'chu want me to do with this?" asked Machi, confused.

"I'm going live! I need you to record this shit. Hezron, hand me that other blunt." Hezron handed Khafre the blunt, stood on the side of Khafre and snatched his Glock 17 out.

"We live," informed Machi, recording Khafre and Hezron.

"Yeah. Yeah! You already know five years day for day, I'm back out'chere! I know a lot of you niggaz want my head, so this what I'ma do for ya. I'ma drop my addy verbally, ya hear me? We live at this bitch ass nigga Kurt grave! Yaaah! We just coolin' smokin' a lil', Kurt!" Khafre fired the blunt up, then pulled his Glock 19. Hezron aimed his Glock 17 at the camera with a devilish grin.

"Come get it, nigga! Come get it, like I told ja!" Khafre taunted. Machi cut the camera, then snatched his Glock 9 from his Tru Religions.

"Dis that shit I live for!" said Hezron with excitement dripping from his voice. "Let me hit that shit," said Hezron, referring to the blunt. Khafre passed the blunt to Hezron and kept his head on swivel.

"I'on think them niggaz coming," proclaimed Machi.

"Give it a few minutes. If nobody don't come in the next ten minutes, we gon' slide," stated Khafre, now high and tipsy but still on point. Kurt was from the projects known as "V-side", but what Khafre and his cousins didn't know was that Kurt had family on 13th street. A tan colored jeep Cherokee conspicuously crept up 12th street, with the window up. In Khafre's mind that was their first mistake. He knew real killers would have pulled up with the windows down blasting. When the occupants of the jeep did attempt to roll the windows down, Khafre, Hezron and Machi all ran towards the jeep. The occupants were hit with a fusillade and attempted to pull off in a hurry, only to crash into a pole a few feet away. The trio advanced on the jeep, never giving the amateur shooters a chance for escape. They emptied the remainder of their clips horridly then ran to the limo.

"Drive!" yelled Hezron. The driver of the limo was a friend of Offtop, so Machi and Hezron weren't worried about him going to the police. He pulled off unconcernedly and blended in with traffic.

Chapter Thirty-Two

Welcome Home

The limo stopped in front of a mansion on Indian River Drive.

"Come on, get out," instructed Machi.

"Who live here?" asked Khafre.

"We do. Our pops bought this house two years ago," said Hezron. The trio climbed out of the limo and traversed up the Syrian Stone driveway. Khafre marveled at the Caribbean architecture and royal palm trees that towered over the multi-hipped roof giving off a tropical feel. They climbed the coral-stoned steps that led to two mahogany and glass doors.

"This shit nice," Khafre admitted, impressed.

"Yeah, pops did his thang," added Machi, ringing the doorbell. Khafre glanced behind him and noticed an Audi parked off to the side in front of a three-car garage.

"Whose whip that is?" questioned Khafre, pointing at the Audi.

"I'on know. Our cars parked inside the garage," exclaimed Hezron. Moments later the door opened.

"Khafre! Welcome home, nephew," greeted Offtop, showing all thirty-two VVs diamonds in his mouth. He had just removed his gold teeth and replaced them a week ago. His dreadlocks hung to his chest, and he was draped in diamonds from his neck to his fingers. Standing 5'6, you could tell Offtop was in shape through the fitted clothes he wore.

"What's good, unk?" asked Khafre, dapping and hugging Offtop.

"I'm glad you made it home. I been to gladiator camp, years ago! That shit real."

"That's an understatement," replied Khafre.

"Y'all come on in, and have a seat. I wanna holla at y'all real quick. When Khafre entered the house, he saw that everything was white and gold. When they all had a seat on the custom hexagonal sectional, he admired the inlaid carpet and linear gas fireplace.

"I'm feelin' what'chu got going on, unk," said Khafre, taking in the ambiance.

"All this here—is in arm's reach. Dedication, persistence, and loyalty can get'chu all this," said Offtop, sparking a blunt.

"What'chu speaking on?" Khafre asked, his curiosity piqued.

"I'ma get to that in a minute. Now, Hezron and Khafre. Y'all wanna tell me why the hell y'all went live on Facebook, holding guns at a nigga grave who you killed?" questioned Offtop, pointing at Khafre. "Everybody knew you killed Kurt and got away wit' it. Why provoke this nigga people?"

"You know I lost my best friend, my Godmother and my father. So, pardon me for not givin' a fuck, unk," Khafre asserted icily. Hezron and Machi looked at Khafre, surprised at his answer.

"That's understandable and I'm sorry for ya loss. But, on some real shit, you gotta start moving with diligence, not off emotion. You hear me?" asked Offtop, blowing smoke from his nose.

"I hear you, unk."

"You listen to me and you'll never have to kill for free again." Khafre nodded in agreement. "Machi, I know you was there too. I just spent all that money gettin' you and Hezron off on that double homicide last summer. I know y'all had somethin' to do wit' them niggaz gettin' killed in that jeep by the graveyard. If them crackaz come wit' that bullshit, it's beatable but damn! Move better! All y'all hear me?"

"Yes, sir," said Hezron and Machi in unison.

"I hear you, unk," added Khafre.

"Khafre, look under the sofa and grab that envelope," Offtop instructed. Khafre reached under the sofa and grabbed the envelope. "Open it." Khafre opened the envelope and saw that it was loaded with all blue-faced hundreds.

"That's for you, nephew. Fifty bands."

"Good lookin', unk," replied Khafre, genuinely grateful.

"Grab them keys off the table right there."

"For what?"

"That Audi AS 68 outside. That's yours, welcome home," said Offtop, smiling.

"Thanks, unk," expressed Khafre, getting up to hug his uncle-in-law.

"I gotta go handle some shit. I'ma link up wit'chu later," Offtop stated, heading to the back of the mansion.

"Fifty-bands and a new whip! Fresh out boy, you already up," affirmed Hezron. Machi just smiled.

"Y'all niggaz already know that was my whip out there?"

"We might have had an idea," laughed Machi. Khafre hugged both of his cousins and promised to link up with them the following day.

***

On the ride to his mother's house, Khafre enjoyed the scenery and the smell of new leather in his whip. He thought about his father, Nilya, and Shenida. Even though it had been half of a decade since their deaths, it all still seemed fresh and surreal. The scene at the graveyard replayed in Khafre's mind, reminding him that he still had the Glock on him. He stopped at Taylor's Creek and dropped it in the inky, murky waters then headed to his mother's. Khafre got out and knocked on the door, a bit nervous. He hadn't seen his mother in five years. Moments later, the door swung open and Shantel's eyes instantly teared up.

"Hey, baby! I missed you so much, boy!" cried Shantel, hugging Khafre's neck.

"Missed you too, mama!" replied Khafre, fighting hard to keep his tears from falling.

"Whose car you got?"

"Unk gave it to me."

"Unk who?"

"Offtop, mama."

"That was nice. What'chu gotta do for it?" questioned Shantel with raised eyebrows.

"It was a welcome home gift, mama. Cool it," laughed Khafre.

"Well, I guess. I love you, boy."

"Love you too, mama."

"You called me with that nonsense, talking 'bout you might not make it home. I see you made it just fine," said Shantel with her hands on her hips.

"Yeah, I had to turn it up on them niggaz, mama."

"I knew you would, Khafre. You got the blood of your father!"

To Be Continued—
Killa Kounty 3
Coming Soon

Lock Down Publications and Ca$h Presents assisted publishing packages.

BASIC PACKAGE $499
Editing
Cover Design
Formatting

UPGRADED PACKAGE $800
Typing
Editing
Cover Design
Formatting

ADVANCE PACKAGE $1,200
Typing
Editing
Cover Design
Formatting
Copyright registration
Proofreading
Upload book to Amazon

LDP SUPREME PACKAGE $1,500
Typing
Editing
Cover Design
Formatting
Copyright registration
Proofreading
Set up Amazon account
Upload book to Amazon
Advertise on LDP Amazon and Facebook page

Khufu

***Other services available upon request. Additional charges
may apply
Lock Down Publications
P.O. Box 944
Stockbridge, GA 30281-9998
Phone # 470 303-9761

Submission Guideline

Submit the first three chapters of your completed manuscript to ldpsubmissions@gmail.com, subject line: Your book's title. The manuscript must be in a .doc file and sent as an attachment. Document should be in Times New Roman, double spaced and in size 12 font. Also, provide your synopsis and full contact information. If sending multiple submissions, they must each be in a separate email.

Have a story but no way to send it electronically? You can still submit to LDP/Ca$h Presents. Send in the first three chapters, written or typed, of your completed manuscript to:

LDP: Submissions Dept
Po Box 944
Stockbridge, Ga 30281

DO NOT send original manuscript. Must be a duplicate.

Provide your synopsis and a cover letter containing your full contact information.

Thanks for considering LDP and Ca$h Presents.

NEW RELEASES

KING OF THE TRENCHES 2 by GHOST & TRANAY AD-
AMS
MOB TIES 5 by SAYNOMORE
KING KILLA by VINCENT "VITTO" HOLLOWAY
JACK BOYS VS DOPE BOYS by ROMELL TUKES
KILLA KOUNTY 2 by KHUFU

KINGPIN KILLAZ IV

STREET KINGS III

PAID IN BLOOD III

CARTEL KILLAZ IV

DOPE GODS III

Hood Rich

SINS OF A HUSTLA II

ASAD

RICH $AVAGE II

MONEY IN THE GRAVE II

By Martell Troublesome Bolden

YAYO V

Bred In The Game 2

S. Allen

CREAM III

By Yolanda Moore

SON OF A DOPE FIEND III

HEAVEN GOT A GHETTO II

By Renta

LOYALTY AIN'T PROMISED III

By Keith Williams

I'M NOTHING WITHOUT HIS LOVE II

SINS OF A THUG II

TO THE THUG I LOVED BEFORE II

By Monet Dragun

QUIET MONEY IV

EXTENDED CLIP III

THUG LIFE IV

By **Trai'Quan**

THE STREETS MADE ME IV

By **Larry D. Wright**

IF YOU CROSS ME ONCE II

By **Anthony Fields**

THE STREETS WILL NEVER CLOSE II

By **K'ajji**

HARD AND RUTHLESS III

THE BILLIONAIRE BENTLEYS II

Von Diesel

KILLA KOUNTY III

By **Khufu**

MONEY GAME III

By **Smoove Dolla**

JACK BOYS VS DOPE BOYS II

By **Romell Tukes**

MURDA WAS THE CASE II

Elijah R. Freeman

THE STREETS NEVER LET GO II

By **Robert Baptiste**

AN UNFORESEEN LOVE III

By **Meesha**

KING OF THE TRENCHES III

by **GHOST & TRANAY ADAMS**

MONEY MAFIA II

LOYAL TO THE SOIL II

By **Jibril Williams**

QUEEN OF THE ZOO II

By **Black Migo**

THE BRICK MAN IV

By **King Rio**

VICIOUS LOYALTY II

Khufu

By Kingpen

A GANGSTA'S PAIN II

By J-Blunt

CONFESSIONS OF A JACKBOY III

By Nicholas Lock

GRIMEY WAYS II

By Ray Vinci

KING KILLA II

By Vincent "Vitto" Holloway

Available Now

RESTRAINING ORDER **I & II**

By **CA$H & Coffee**

LOVE KNOWS NO BOUNDARIES **I II & III**

By **Coffee**

RAISED AS A GOON I, II, III & IV

BRED BY THE SLUMS I, II, III

BLAST FOR ME I & II

ROTTEN TO THE CORE I II III

A BRONX TALE I, II, III

DUFFLE BAG CARTEL I II III IV V VI

HEARTLESS GOON I II III IV V

A SAVAGE DOPEBOY I II

DRUG LORDS I II III

CUTTHROAT MAFIA I II

KING OF THE TRENCHES

By **Ghost**

LAY IT DOWN **I & II**

LAST OF A DYING BREED I II

BLOOD STAINS OF A SHOTTA I & II III

By **Jamaica**

LOYAL TO THE GAME I II III

LIFE OF SIN I, II III

By **TJ & Jelissa**

BLOODY COMMAS I & II

SKI MASK CARTEL I II & III

KING OF NEW YORK I II,III IV V

RISE TO POWER I II III

COKE KINGS I II III IV V

BORN HEARTLESS I II III IV

KING OF THE TRAP I II

By **T.J. Edwards**

IF LOVING HIM IS WRONG…I & II

LOVE ME EVEN WHEN IT HURTS I II III

By **Jelissa**

WHEN THE STREETS CLAP BACK I & II III

THE HEART OF A SAVAGE I II III

MONEY MAFIA

LOYAL TO THE SOIL

By **Jibril Williams**

A DISTINGUISHED THUG STOLE MY HEART I II & III

LOVE SHOULDN'T HURT I II III IV

RENEGADE BOYS I II III IV

Khufu

PAID IN KARMA I II III

SAVAGE STORMS I II

AN UNFORESEEN LOVE I II

By **Meesha**

A GANGSTER'S CODE I &, II III

A GANGSTER'S SYN I II III

THE SAVAGE LIFE I II III

CHAINED TO THE STREETS I II III

BLOOD ON THE MONEY I II III

A GANGSTA'S PAIN

By J-Blunt

PUSH IT TO THE LIMIT

By **Bre' Hayes**

BLOOD OF A BOSS **I, II, III, IV, V**

SHADOWS OF THE GAME

TRAP BASTARD

By **Askari**

THE STREETS BLEED MURDER **I, II & III**

THE HEART OF A GANGSTA I II& III

By **Jerry Jackson**

CUM FOR ME I II III IV V VI VII VIII

An **LDP Erotica Collaboration**

BRIDE OF A HUSTLA **I II & II**

THE FETTI GIRLS **I, II& III**

CORRUPTED BY A GANGSTA I, II III, IV

BLINDED BY HIS LOVE

THE PRICE YOU PAY FOR LOVE I, II ,III

DOPE GIRL MAGIC I II III

By **Destiny Skai**

WHEN A GOOD GIRL GOES BAD

By **Adrienne**
THE COST OF LOYALTY I II III
By Kweli
A GANGSTER'S REVENGE **I II III & IV**
THE BOSS MAN'S DAUGHTERS I II III IV V
A SAVAGE LOVE **I & II**
BAE BELONGS TO ME I II
A HUSTLER'S DECEIT I, II, III
WHAT BAD BITCHES DO I, II, III
SOUL OF A MONSTER I II III
KILL ZONE
A DOPE BOY'S QUEEN I II III
By **Aryanna**
A KINGPIN'S AMBITON
A KINGPIN'S AMBITION **II**
I MURDER FOR THE DOUGH
By **Ambitious**
TRUE SAVAGE I II III IV V VI VII
DOPE BOY MAGIC I, II, III
MIDNIGHT CARTEL I II III
CITY OF KINGZ I II
NIGHTMARE ON SILENT AVE
THE PLUG OF LIL MEXICO II

By **Chris Green**
A DOPEBOY'S PRAYER
By **Eddie "Wolf" Lee**
THE KING CARTEL **I, II & III**
By **Frank Gresham**
THESE NIGGAS AIN'T LOYAL **I, II & III**

Khufu

By **Nikki Tee**
GANGSTA SHYT **I II &III**
By **CATO**
THE ULTIMATE BETRAYAL
By **Phoenix**
BOSS'N UP **I , II & III**
By **Royal Nicole**
I LOVE YOU TO DEATH
By **Destiny J**
I RIDE FOR MY HITTA
I STILL RIDE FOR MY HITTA
By **Misty Holt**
LOVE & CHASIN' PAPER
By **Qay Crockett**
TO DIE IN VAIN
SINS OF A HUSTLA
By **ASAD**
BROOKLYN HUSTLAZ
By **Boogsy Morina**
BROOKLYN ON LOCK I & II
By **Sonovia**
GANGSTA CITY
By **Teddy Duke**
A DRUG KING AND HIS DIAMOND I & II III
A DOPEMAN'S RICHES
HER MAN, MINE'S TOO I, II
CASH MONEY HO'S
THE WIFEY I USED TO BE I II
By Nicole Goosby
TRAPHOUSE KING **I II & III**

KINGPIN KILLAZ I II III

STREET KINGS I II

PAID IN BLOOD **I II**

CARTEL KILLAZ I II III

DOPE GODS I II

By **Hood Rich**

LIPSTICK KILLAH **I, II, III**

CRIME OF PASSION I II & III

FRIEND OR FOE I II III

By **Mimi**

STEADY MOBBN' **I, II, III**

THE STREETS STAINED MY SOUL I II III

By **Marcellus Allen**

WHO SHOT YA **I, II, III**

SON OF A DOPE FIEND I II

HEAVEN GOT A GHETTO

Renta

GORILLAZ IN THE BAY **I II III IV**

TEARS OF A GANGSTA I II

3X KRAZY I II

STRAIGHT BEAST MODE

DE'KARI

TRIGGADALE I II III

MURDAROBER WAS THE CASE

Elijah R. Freeman

GOD BLESS THE TRAPPERS I, II, III

THESE SCANDALOUS STREETS I, II, III

FEAR MY GANGSTA I, II, III IV, V

THESE STREETS DON'T LOVE NOBODY I, II

BURY ME A G I, II, III, IV, V

A GANGSTA'S EMPIRE I, II, III, IV

THE DOPEMAN'S BODYGAURD I II

THE REALEST KILLAZ I II III

THE LAST OF THE OGS I II III

Tranay Adams

THE STREETS ARE CALLING

Duquie Wilson

MARRIED TO A BOSS I II III

By Destiny Skai & Chris Green

KINGZ OF THE GAME I II III IV V VI

Playa Ray

SLAUGHTER GANG I II III

RUTHLESS HEART I II III

By Willie Slaughter

FUK SHYT

By Blakk Diamond

DON'T F#CK WITH MY HEART I II

By Linnea

ADDICTED TO THE DRAMA I II III

IN THE ARM OF HIS BOSS II

By Jamila

YAYO I II III IV

A SHOOTER'S AMBITION I II

BRED IN THE GAME

By S. Allen

TRAP GOD I II III

RICH $AVAGE

MONEY IN THE GRAVE I II

By Martell Troublesome Bolden

FOREVER GANGSTA

GLOCKS ON SATIN SHEETS I II

By Adrian Dulan

TOE TAGZ I II III

LEVELS TO THIS SHYT I II

By Ah'Million

KINGPIN DREAMS I II III

By Paper Boi Rari

CONFESSIONS OF A GANGSTA I II III IV

CONFESSIONS OF A JACKBOY I II

By Nicholas Lock

I'M NOTHING WITHOUT HIS LOVE

SINS OF A THUG

TO THE THUG I LOVED BEFORE

A GANGSTA SAVED XMAS

By Monet Dragun

CAUGHT UP IN THE LIFE I II III

THE STREETS NEVER LET GO

By Robert Baptiste

NEW TO THE GAME I II III

MONEY, MURDER & MEMORIES I II III

By **Malik D. Rice**

LIFE OF A SAVAGE I II III

A GANGSTA'S QUR'AN I II III

MURDA SEASON I II III

GANGLAND CARTEL I II III

CHI'RAQ GANGSTAS I II III

KILLERS ON ELM STREET I II III

JACK BOYZ N DA BRONX I II III

A DOPEBOY'S DREAM I II III

JACK BOYS VS DOPE BOYS

Khufu

By **Romell Tukes**
LOYALTY AIN'T PROMISED I II
By **Keith Williams**
QUIET MONEY I II III
THUG LIFE I II III
EXTENDED CLIP I II
By **Trai'Quan**
THE STREETS MADE ME I II III
By **Larry D. Wright**
THE ULTIMATE SACRIFICE I, II, III, IV, V, VI
KHADIFI
IF YOU CROSS ME ONCE
ANGEL I II
IN THE BLINK OF AN EYE
By **Anthony Fields**
THE LIFE OF A HOOD STAR
By **Ca$h & Rashia Wilson**
THE STREETS WILL NEVER CLOSE
By **K'ajji**
CREAM I II
By **Yolanda Moore**
NIGHTMARES OF A HUSTLA I II III
By **King Dream**
CONCRETE KILLA I II
VICIOUS LOYALTY
By **Kingpen**
HARD AND RUTHLESS I II
MOB TOWN 251
THE BILLIONAIRE BENTLEYS
By **Von Diesel**

GHOST MOB

Stilloan Robinson

MOB TIES I II III IV V

By SayNoMore

BODYMORE MURDERLAND I II III

By Delmont Player

FOR THE LOVE OF A BOSS

By C. D. Blue

MOBBED UP I II III IV

THE BRICK MAN I II III

By King Rio

KILLA KOUNTY I II

By Khufu

MONEY GAME I II

By Smoove Dolla

A GANGSTA'S KARMA I II

By FLAME

KING OF THE TRENCHES I II

by **GHOST & TRANAY ADAMS**

QUEEN OF THE ZOO

By **Black Migo**

GRIMEY WAYS

By Ray Vinci

XMAS WITH AN ATL SHOOTER

By Ca$h & Destiny Skai

KING KILLA

By Vincent "Vitto" Holloway

BOOKS BY LDP'S CEO, CA$H

TRUST IN NO MAN

TRUST IN NO MAN 2

TRUST IN NO MAN 3

BONDED BY BLOOD

SHORTY GOT A THUG

THUGS CRY

THUGS CRY 2

THUGS CRY 3

TRUST NO BITCH

TRUST NO BITCH 2

TRUST NO BITCH 3

TIL MY CASKET DROPS

RESTRAINING ORDER

RESTRAINING ORDER 2

IN LOVE WITH A CONVICT

LIFE OF A HOOD STAR

XMAS WITH AN ATL SHOOTER

Killa Kounty 2

CPSIA information can be obtained
at www.ICGtesting.com
Printed in the USA
LVHW011146200322
713909LV00010B/1017